D0742817

WILD TURKEY

WILD TURKEY

Michael Hemmingson

A TOM DOHERTY ASSOCIATES BOOK
NEW YORK

This is a work of fiction. All the characters and events portrayed in this novel are either fictitious or are used fictitiously.

WILD TURKEY

Copyright © 2001 by Michael Hemmingson

This book is printed on acid-free paper.

Design by Jane Adele Regina

A Forge Book
Published by Tom Doherty Associates, LLC
175 Fifth Avenue
New York, NY 10010

www.tor.com

Forge® is a registered trademark of Tom Doherty Associates, LLC.

Library of Congress Cataloging-in-Publication Data

Hemmingson, Michael A.
    Wild turkey / Michael Hemmingson.—1st ed.
      p. cm.
    "A Tom Doherty Associates book."
    ISBN 0-312-87873-7 (alk. paper)
      1. Househusbands—Fiction. 2. Neighborhood—Fiction. 3. Unemployed—Fiction. I. Title.
PS3558.E479154 W55 2001
813'.54—dc21

2001018959

First Edition: May 2001

Printed in the United States of America

0 9 8 7 6 5 4 3 2 1

for Christine Doyle

From then on, strange things happened to me.

—Paul Auster, *Moon Palace*

recall this particular married woman I'd had a short fling with when I was in my mid-twenties. I'd met her at the opening of an art exhibit in downtown San Diego in the Gaslamp Quarter; she was thirty-four and her name was Barbara. She was one of the would-be dancer-painter types that always seemed to be friends with my ex-girlfriend, Elaine. I'd actually gone to the exhibit at the Rita Dear Gallery hoping to spark something up with Elaine again, as we occasionally did, being off-and-on for the past several years. I was immediately drawn to Barbara—her pale skin and dark hair, her lithe body. She wasn't wearing a ring and I didn't know she was married until Elaine said, "We have to meet Barbara's husband and some friends at this restaurant at eight, you should come." As with all gallery openings, there was plenty of wine, and someone brought out spiked punch, and vodka Jell-O. Barbara quickly got drunk; as we talked, she kept leaning into me and touching my arm, and then my chest. Someone put on loud music. As I tried to have a conversation with Barbara, she leaned over and said into my ear, her tongue touching my flesh, "The music is too loud, let's talk outside." We went outside. She pointed to a Toyota Camry and said, "That's my car," and the next thing I knew, we were in the back of her car and necking. It was pretty intense. She stopped, a hand on my chest. "I can't do this," she said, "I'm married."

"Okay."

"And Elaine and I are late. My husband's going to worry."

"You're all right."

"Not to drive."

"The restaurant isn't far. Walk."

"Come with us," she said.

"I don't think so."

"Please," she said.

I said, "All right."

I walked Elaine and Barbara to the restaurant. It was eight-thirty but her husband—a thick man in a suit—didn't seem worried, didn't seem to notice the time. He was deep in conversation with several other men and women in suits, talking about bonds and securities and real estate.

I felt uncomfortable, observing Barbara kiss her husband lightly on the lips, hanging onto his thick arm.

They ordered dinner.

After one drink, I left—abruptly. I said there was something I forgot to attend to. Barbara gave me a look I didn't understand. I didn't want to understand it.

I lived in a downtown studio a few blocks away: I, the starving law student. I went home, turned on the TV. I was sad.

An hour later: a knock on my door.

Barbara, still drunk, came right in. She smelled nice.

"I have twenty, maybe thirty minutes," she said. Her eyes were glassy. "My husband and I took separate cars, I'm sure you know. But if I don't get home in time, he'll worry."

I was flabbergasted. "How did you know where I lived?"

"Elaine told me—"

"She—"

"Doesn't have a clue," Barbara said. The woman didn't waste any time; she pulled me to her and kissed me. We quickly undressed and went to my futon.

"Look," she said. "I want you to know I've never done anything like this, *ever*. I've never had an affair."

"Never?"

"Ten years of marriage, never."

"Your husband?"

"I don't think so."

"You love him?"

"Very much."

"So why—"

"Don't ask why," Barbara said, "just screw me, okay?"

She wasn't my first married woman, and not my last. I'd heard all the excuses for infidelity since I was nineteen and had discovered the sad and sexual world of married women. Barbara and I fucked twice in an hour and a half of loss, bliss, and body parts—clearly well over her time limit.

"It's late," she said, her head on my chest.

"Will he be waiting?"

"He probably went straight to bed, like he always does. He won't notice."

"He trusts you."

"He just doesn't notice. I should go," but she didn't move.

I said, "Stay."

She sat up, looking for her clothes. "That I can't do."

I watched her slip her panties and bra on, then her black jeans and gray vest. I felt hollow.

I saw her to the door.

"Bye," she said.

I grabbed her arm. She smiled. I said, "Hey." I kissed her. It was a ten-minute kiss.

"Hey, boy," she said.

"Back to bed?" I said.

"I'm scared," she said, "I'm married," and she pushed me away, and she ran.

I think I understood what she was going through.

Well, if I didn't then, I do now.

I felt the same way, more than ten years later, when I was unfaithful to my wife, Tina—when I embarked on my disastrous affair with Cassandra Payne.

I was thirty-eight and had been married to Tina for five years. We were doing the American Suburban routine—tract house in San Diego, two children (a boy and a girl), two cars, good jobs . . . until I lost mine.

After graduating law school, I did a year as a public defender, then got hired at a fairly decent law firm as a junior litigator. For three years, I never went to trial, hardly walked into a court except for motion hearings. Most civil lawsuits wind up in a settlement at some point, or remain in limbo. But when I finally did go to trial, on a pretty large medical malpractice suit, I lost the case, and my employer was out half a million dollars, having taken the case on contingency. The partners let me go.

I got a job at another, less prestigious firm. A lot of ambulance chasing was going on there; I was expected to do just that. It was the last thing I wanted in my life. I didn't go to law school for this, and it hurt, it deeply pained me, and I dreaded getting up each morning, trying to force settlements out of insurance companies and various institutions. One day, something inside me snapped. I was at a motion-to-strike hearing; the opposing counsel had put together an effective line of bullshit. The next thing I knew, I had this attorney on the floor of the courtroom, right in front of the judge's bench, and I was choking the poor unsuspecting bastard.

The bailiff pulled me away and cuffed me; I was arrested and sent through the system. At this point I could better understand the situation of some of my clients. Tina had to bail me out; the firm I worked at wouldn't spend a dime. I was charged with assault and battery, I was fired, and the other lawyer sued me. I pleaded no contest, and because I had no record, was given a hundred hours of community service, probation, and a fine. The lawsuit was still waiting to go to trial; I refused to settle and I didn't think the lawyer was going to pursue it any further. In the meantime, the State Bar was investigating the matter.

I briefly went into private practice, operating out of my home, but I screwed things up, not paying attention to details, and a client of mine sued me for legal malpractice and complained to the bar. I settled with my ex-client for $3,000, and then, based on all of the above, was disbarred for a period of five years.

All wasn't lost, however. While I was doing well, I had made some smart investments with decent returns, and Tina had a good job working for Social Security, evaluating SSI eligibility. She'd been working part time, then went to full time.

We came to this agreement: since the returns on the investments would keep us in the same lifestyle for a few years, her job would supplement, add extra security. While I figured out what I was going to do, I would become a house husband. Our son, Matthew, was starting kindergarten. Our daughter, Jessica, was just getting out of diapers. I would do the laundry, keep the house clean, mow the lawn, and have dinner ready when she came home.

This wasn't so bad. I needed the sabbatical. I don't know what went wrong. I had always wanted to be a lawyer, ever since I was a kid and watched reruns of *Perry Mason*. I'd worked hard to get through law school and pass the bar exam. I worked very hard to rise in the profession. I guess the pressure was too much.

Maybe I would return to practice when I could get my license back, maybe I wouldn't. Maybe I would write novels about lawyers like John Grisham. Maybe I'd become a lumberjack or a fireman. I figured my options were wide open and I had plenty of time to figure things out.

I had a beautiful wife. I had two wonderful children. I had a fine, comfortable home, with an increasing market value. I had a nice car. My days were without stress: in the morning, I made Tina and the children breakfast. I kissed Tina goodbye. I helped Matthew get ready for school. I drove Matthew to school, Jessica with me. Jessica and I returned home. She watched cartoons and I opened a beer. I read, or watched cartoons. I did the laundry. I mowed the lawn. I picked up Matthew from school and brought him home, and he watched afternoon cartoons with his little sister. I had a beer. Sometimes, I'd have beers with other men in the neighborhood, men who soon became my friends.

There were two such men who figure in this story. One was Bryan Vaughn, a fifty-seven-year-old police veteran. He used to be a detective. The other was David Larson, part-time college professor. David was a baseball fanatic, and so was Bryan. In fact, they were both members of an amateur local team, a team I wound up joining.

My friendship with both of these men would help change my life forever.

When you have time on your hands, and you're outside, you start noticing a lot about the block you live on. It becomes an entity all its own. There are the intricate nuances, the upset balance if someone (like the mailman, or the trash collector) doesn't maintain a previous routine.

Before, I'd never really noticed the neighborhood or my neighbors, always absorbed with my work and hardly home. I don't know why I hadn't taken prior heed of Cassandra Payne. I'd seen her, briefly, but hadn't *noticed* her. Being career-minded and married, I'd forgotten what it was like simply to look upon another woman's beauty with admiration and desire.

There was much to admire and desire about Cassandra Payne. She was tall and slender, almost six feet, with fine pale skin and shoulder-length, straight, jet-black hair. She had very long and agile legs, which I started to closely scrutinize as she came to and from her house. She often wore miniskirts; usually black or white, sometimes leather, sometimes cotton. Once, she wore a yellow cotton mini, and as she got into her car (a Ford Taurus) I caught a glimpse—at least I think I did, from my vantage point across the street—of matching yellow underwear. This isn't to say that she always wore miniskirts—sometimes she wore long skirts, or skorts, or slacks or jeans.

It started to become a game for me, catching her leaving the house and getting into her car, hearing her car (which had a distinctive sound, like it would need a new muffler soon) coming down the street. I'd watch her from the porch, or the window, or with Bryan and David as we sat around and had beers.

This story appropriately begins the day I caught my son Matthew setting the trash can on fire.

I smelled something burning through the window. I went outside. The smell was coming from the side of the house. I went to inspect. There my son was, gazing with rapt attention at the flames dancing out of the metal trash can.

"Matthew!" I yelled, and grabbed him, lifting him in my arms, saving him from harm's way.

I put him the middle of the yard, quickly grabbed the garden hose and turned the water on—rushed to the can, and put out the burning newspapers and milk cartons and junk mail.

My son stood at my side, witnessing his precious fire vanish. He looked disappointed.

"How did this happen?" I asked no one, and to Matthew: "How did that fire happen?"

He shrugged.

I saw the matches in his hand.

"Did you start that fire?" I said.

He just looked at me.

I leaned down and grabbed him by the shoulders. "Matthew, why? Why would you do such a thing?" I was shaking him, probably a little too hard.

He looked like he was going to cry. "I wanted to see!"

"Where did you get such an idea?"

"Paulie."

"Paulie. Who's Paulie?"

"At school."

"Look," I started to say, and that's when I noticed the woman in the house across the street from me walk out the door. She was in a black leather mini and fishnet stockings. The mini barely covered what was beyond her hips. She stopped to adjust her shoe, just before getting into the Taurus, and I thought—oh my—I saw something I shouldn't have. She was wearing a white blouse, the fabric so thin I could make out her black bra. She got into her car, put on a pair of sunglasses, and drove off.

"Daddy?" my son said.

I took the matches away. "Don't ever, ever do that again," I told him. "Come on," and I put my hand on his head, gently; we went back into our home.

I was never a baseball fan, not as a kid, and not as an adult. I vaguely recall being in Little League and hating the outfit—the long socks, the pants, the hat, the whole thing. I was a bad player, too, always placed way out in left field, and hardly ever hitting the ball when I went up to bat. But there I was, thirty-eight-years-old, disbarred and unemployed, and I was playing baseball every Saturday afternoon with a bunch of middle-aged men who should've known better.

At first, I just went to watch the games; David was the pitcher and Bryan acted as a sort of quasi coach, barking out orders like this all meant something. It was a good excuse to get out of the house, kick back, and drink beer, watching these heavy-in-the-middle, balding, and squinty-eyed men play.

It was amusing, to say the least.

The bleachers were never very full at the park, mostly wives and children, a few friends, a few kids from the neighborhood who would heckle and yell, "You can hit a ball farther than that, old man!" or "Run, pops, run!"

One day, as the story goes, they lost a player—the fellow had a minor heart attack at home, so he wouldn't be back on the field. Bryan and David suggested I fill in the spot.

"I don't play baseball," I said.

"Everyone plays baseball," David said. "It's the all-American sport!"

"I don't play well," I said.

"Neither does anyone else on the team," Bryan said.

He had a point. I figured, what the hell, why not. They got

me a uniform—the team was called the Fritzes, of all things—
and a hat, and I was ready to play.

Tina thought I was being silly, "men acting like boys" she
said; yet I knew she was relieved that I would be getting out
in the sun and engaging in some much needed exercise.

To my surprise, I enjoyed that first game. There wasn't the
pressure of Little League—where you felt examined, where
you knew your parents were watching from the stands, hoping
you'd dazzle everyone, only to fail; where other boys on the
team—those who could play—would ridicule you for mess-
ups. Out here, among the middle-aged, it didn't matter if you
screwed up. No one was a star, and no one was passing judg-
ment. If you didn't catch a ball, or if you struck out, it was,
"Darn, better luck next time." Not only that, we drank beer
in the dugout. When Bryan asked me, after the game (which
we lost 12-7), if I wanted to be a permanent member of the
Fritzes, I said yes.

Now that I was an amateur baseball player, I felt I had a
new purpose. I was energized. After five months of being
cooped up in the house, I was starting to think of the future
again. On Monday, I told myself I'd look into getting a job;
part-time, perhaps, or maybe something temporary, but *something.*

That night, I vigorously made love to Tina. I marveled at
my own randy stamina and succeeding erection. So did Tina.

"Where is all this energy coming from?" she asked after the
second time.

"You don't like?"

"I love it," she said. "I'm just wondering—"

"Just feeling horny," I said, my mouth on hers.

"So I noticed, cowboy."

Our sex life had dwindled quite a bit. I didn't realize this
until that night. It's the way with husbands and wives, married
five years.

I thought we'd get back to more regular sex after that. I was wrong.

We got married in Las Vegas, by the way. It should have been somewhere else. Las Vegas is a curse for me.

Bryan lived next door. The first time I met him, I was mowing the lawn. Or trying to. The lawn mower kept dying, and I had trouble restarting it.

"Problem?"

He was standing on his neatly mowed lawn, in shorts and a T-shirt, holding a glass. He wore a floppy canvas fishing cap. He was five-foot-nine, heavyset at two hundred and seventy pounds, I'd say. Pale blue eyes and ruddy cheeks. Think the Skipper from *Gilligan's Island*, but with more style.

"Damn thing keeps dying," I said.

"Let me take a look."

When he passed by me, I smelled vodka from his glass. He seemed like an all right kind of guy. He took one look at my lawn mower, fiddled with the engine a bit, stood up and said, "Yeah, that's what I thought." He was holding something small and cylindrical in his hand. "Fried spark plug. When's the last time you changed it?"

"Never have," I told him. "Never thought I needed to."

"You change the spark plugs in your car, don't you?"

"My mechanic does that every six months."

"You gotta do it once a year with mowers. How long have you had this one?"

"Not sure," I said, and I really didn't know. I think we bought it when Tina and I got the house. "Three years."

"Well, there you go. I just might have the spark plug to fit the bill. I'll be back in a sec." He walked over to his garage door, opened it, and went inside. I stood next to my dead lawn mower like an idiot. He came back, smiling, drinking from his glass. He placed the new spark plug in my lawn mower and said, "Okay, son, give her a whirl."

No one had called me "son" in a long time, except for one

of the senior partners in the first firm I worked for. I felt a pang of nostalgia, and an ache for my first major fuck-up. My own father had never called me "son." It was usually "kid" or "brat."

I hit the button, and the mower started, and it *purred.*

"Damn," I said.

"Good as new," he said.

"Thanks," I said, over the purring engine. I held out my hand. "Philip Lansdale."

He shook my hand. He had a very tight grip. "Bryan Vaughn."

I mowed my front yard and Bryan Vaughn went back to his porch; he sat in a rocking chair, fresh glass in hand, and watched nothing—maybe the clouds in the sky and the occasional passing airplane. I didn't do a good job with the lawn, at least not as good as Vaughn kept his, or many of the other neighborhood lawns.

When I was a kid, I never cared for the task. The smell of grass often made my nose itch, and sometimes I'd sneeze. Tina used to do this chore, when I was working during the day; she said she loved yard work. She could have it back as far as I was concerned.

When I was done, and I put the mower away in the garage, Bryan Vaughn called out, "How'd she do for you, kid?"

Kid. "Great," I replied. "Thanks again."

"Hey, no problem."

I hesitated and said, "How about a beer?"

"In town, or here?"

"Well, here, my children are inside."

"Sure," he said, "why the hell not? I like beer just like any other guy."

And vodka. But I hadn't started to touch the hard booze yet—not yet, not until later.

Bryan came over, and I got out the good stuff, Samuel Adams. I thought it would be rude to give a man who'd given me a new spark plug a Budweiser. I had some white plastic lawn chairs I placed out front, and we sat down with our beers. His glass of vodka was still half full, which he sipped at from time to time, chasing it down with beer.

"My lawn looks like crap," I finally said.

"Nah," he said. "It's okay."

"Yours is so neat and perfect. How do you do it?"

"There's this enterprising young fellow—eleven years old— comes around every Saturday. I pay him ten bucks. He goes from house to house. Bet the kid clears a good one, two hundred a weekend. I like kids who know how to work and make a buck. That kid'll go far."

That didn't make me feel any better. "Send him over here next time."

He laughed.

"What's ten bucks," I said, "between a nice lawn and a crappy one."

"It's not like anyone looks at lawns around here," he said.

I was looking, all of the sudden.

"People don't look at much anymore," he went on. "They don't see what's in front of them. They don't see the people around them. They don't pay attention. Always busy, going here, there. Wouldn't you say?"

"I guess so." I knew what he meant.

"It's sad. But hell, it's the way it is, right?"

"Right."

We opened two more beers.

My daughter, Jessica, came out, crying. Matthew wouldn't let her watch the cartoon she wanted to watch.

"Matthew!" I yelled. "It's your sister's hour! Let her watch her show!"

I sent her back in. She seemed happy now.

"Sweet little girl," Bryan Vaughn said.

"Yeah. She is. How long have you lived on this block?"

"Hell," he said. "Fifteen years, I'd say."

"And we've never met before," I said, like it was a surprise. We both knew it wasn't.

"I've met your wife, Tina, any number of times. Back when she was around more. Now she's always gone, and you're here."

"She's the full-time worker now," I said, feeling some shame admitting that. He didn't know that I had plenty of cash reserve from the investments; my statement probably sounded like I was lazy and my poor wife had to go out and earn the bacon. But his face didn't register any opinion or disapproval; it didn't register anything. And why should I care what he thought, anyway? I added, "I'm between jobs."

"Good to take a break now and then. I gather you used to be busy, you were always coming and going in such a rush."

I nodded.

He said, "What did you do before?"

"I was a lawyer."

"Oh! Oh my!" He laughed and clutched his chest. "There was a time when I used to wanna shoot every lawyer in town."

"Well don't shoot me, I'm a lawyer in the past tense," I said. "What did you do?"

"I was a cop," he said, drinking, looking at the sky. "Cop for thirty years. Detective in vice when I retired. But I worked narcotics and homicide. Didn't like corpses, killers, and drug dealers; so I stuck with pimps, prostitutes, and kiddy-porn pushers. Now I hear you get it all over the Internet, never have to leave your house. As for lawyers—damn slimy cheap lawyers and public defenders always getting their clients off on bullcrap: warrant not worded properly, rights weren't read, violation of—what was it? How did they say it? 'Procedural due process.' But hell, that's all in the past now. Lawyers gotta make money like anyone else. What kind of criminal did you defend?"

"I wasn't that kind of lawyer," I said. "Civil litigation." I didn't bother to tell him that I started off in the public defender's office and defended every kind of petty criminal and thug you could imagine.

"You mean lawsuits?" he said.

"Yeah," I said.

"Bullshit lawsuits?" he said.

"Sometimes they're bullshit," I said, "sometimes they're sincere."

He smiled. "Well, I won't hold it against you. You seem like a good person."

I wondered if I was a good person. I *was* then, at any rate.

Tina's car pulled into the driveway.

"Little lady's home," Bryan said.

"Yeah," I said. She was early. I had a bad thought that maybe she got fired. We'd be two unemployed people, staying home all day. That didn't sound too bad. I realized I hadn't started dinner, and at this point I think I was too buzzed. Bryan and I were on the second six-pack of Samuel Adams and the alcohol was already starting to affect me.

"Boys," Tina said, looking at us with a *tsk-tsk* quietly on her lips.

"Mrs. Lansdale," Bryan nodded. "How've you been?"

"Busy busy," she said. "What are you boys up to?"

He said, "Drinking beers and shooting baloney like manly men do."

"I see."

"You're home early," I said.

"Can't I come home early once in a while?" Tina said. "I don't want to keep a routine. I'll be too predictable. You'll start bringing women around if you think I'll always come back at the same time."

"I didn't start dinner," I said sheepishly. "Maybe we could go out. Taco Bell. Jack in the Box."

"Burger King," she said. "You know the kids'll want Burger King."

She went inside.

"My wife works too," Bryan said. "Ellen. You probably haven't met her."

"No."

"You will. She works down at the library. Downtown. Loves books. She doesn't need to work, my pension does us fine. But she loves the library, and she loves books."

"I made money off some investments," I blurted out. I guess I wanted him to know that Tina wasn't bringing home all the bread and butter.

"Good to have securities," was his reply to that.

"Well," I said, "it won't always be there."

"If I was smart, when I was your age, I would've invested in computers. Computers were a joke twenty years ago. Thirty even. Now look, they run the world."

I didn't tell him my investments had been on World Wide Web companies, back when people thought those were a joke as well.

Tina came out with the children—Jessica in her arms, Matthew next to her. "Off to Burger King," she said. "What's your order?"

"The usual," I said.

"The usual it is," she said.

She piled herself and the kids into her car and they drove off.

"Nice to have a family," Bryan Vaughn said, nodding, looking at the sky, drinking his beer.

"You have any children?" I asked.

"I did. Two daughters." He shook his head. "The oldest, Donna, she committed suicide at thirteen. Over a boy who dumped her. Slit her wrists and neck, I found her that night in the tub, same day I found two dead children in a car while on the job." He said this so calmly, like he was reading a report of someone else's life. "That was the day I quit homicide," he added. "My youngest, Rachel, she left home at nineteen, and I haven't heard from her since. That was ten years ago. She hates me and I don't know why. Something about being a cop. A lot of anger in that girl. I don't know if she's alive or dead, she'll never contact me or her mother, this I know, so I figure . . ." He didn't finish. His voice had cracked.

I felt weird. I couldn't imagine a future without Matthew and Jessica. "I'm sorry."

"Hell, I've gotten over it," he said. I didn't believe him. "Ellen hasn't. That's why she likes books so much. Books are always the same. They're always with you. Those are her words."

liked Bryan Vaughn, and he seemed to like me as well, and, soon enough, we became good friends. Basically, all we did was sit around at his place or mine, drinking and talking. He had a lot of great stories about the police force, many of which turned out to be violent and sad.

I soon became friends with David Larson too. He lived in the house next to Bryan's. David taught political science part-time at San Diego State University. He would get home around one in the afternoon, take a nap, and join Bryan and me at around three.

It got to be that each morning I'd get up and look forward to getting drunk with my newfound friends. I took Matthew to school, Jessica always found something to entertain herself with, or she'd nap, or she'd just play on the grass while we men lounged about. I started to become lax in my house duties, but Tina didn't seem to notice or didn't mention it. She was too caught up, now, in the world of full-time work.

On weekends, the three of us would sometimes get together for the rap-and-drink session, but this was usually short. Bryan's wife was home, and she liked him to pay attention to her. David didn't have a wife or a girlfriend; he liked to read books.

On Saturdays, of course, there was baseball.

I told Bryan that I thought David was gay. "He's never mentioned any women in his past," Bryan said. "And he certainly doesn't have any women now. I hear these college professors always get laid by the young girls in their classes. Father-figure or authority-figure thing. Rachel ran away with a forty-year-old man, you know."

"I didn't," I said.

"She did," he said.

"Maybe he is screwing some students, but keeps a lid on it," Bryan said. "That sort of thing can get you fired, and he doesn't have tenure."

"Maybe."

"I *don't* think he's gay," Bryan said.

"Would it matter if he was?"

"I guess not," he said.

I knew that David didn't make enough as a part-time professor to live in a two-story suburban home. He told us, one day, that the house belonged to his mother, and when she died, he inherited it. There was no doubt about David's sexual orientation the day we all saw Cassandra Payne come home in a rush.

She was driving her Taurus down the street fast, and tore into the driveway of her house, tires screeching. Bryan, David, and I were on my porch, and we stopped talking at once. She hurried out of her car, sunglasses on, wearing tight blue jeans and a halter. She opened her front door and left it ajar.

Bryan raised his eyebrows and said, "Some people lead such hasty lives."

David twitched in his chair.

Several minutes later, she came back out, this time wearing a short gray skirt and fumbling with the buttons of a pale blue blouse. I caught a glimpse of a dark bra, and her white skin, as she was trying to button the blouse, tuck it in the skirt, and get back into the car.

This sight, needless to say, had an erotic effect: the skin, the clothes, the bare legs, the high heels clacking on the cement of the driveway.

She drove away as fast as she arrived.

"She's going to get a ticket," Bryan said.

"She's too *gorgeous* to get a ticket," David said.

"Yeah," Bryan said. "One glance at her, a traffic cop'll tear the ticket up."

"Who is she?" I said.

"You don't know your own neighbors?" David said, like he was amused. He also seemed suddenly quite nervous.

Bryan laughed. "Sometimes, I bet, Philip doesn't even know his own last name."

I had to think about that one. He was kidding, of course, but it struck a sensitive chord in me. I tried not to let it show.

David said, "Her name is Cassandra Payne. And that's all I know about her," he added quickly. "I don't even know her husband's first name."

"Lawrence," said Bryan.

"I've seen her once or twice," I admitted. "But not the husband."

"He keeps odd hours," Bryan said. "Out of town a lot. England, I think."

"England," I said.

"They're Brits, both of them. Great accents, just like Roger Moore or something."

"David Niven," said David.

"I've talked briefly with both of them," Bryan said, "but I don't know squat about their lives."

"But she's a looker," said David.

"You got *that* right," said Bryan, smiling wide. "Did you get a load of those *legs*?"

"Yeah," I said.

"Not much in the tit department, but who cares?"

"And that ass," David said.

"I didn't get a glimpse of her ass," Bryan said. He was lying.

"She has a nice ass."

"That I wouldn't doubt."

"Well," David said, like he knew, "she does."

"How old do you think she is?" I asked. "Thirty?"

"I'd say a few years younger," Bryan said.

"How can you tell?" asked David.

Bryan said, "I used to be a cop. I can tell these things. And she likes older men, because Lawrence Payne is at least fifty."

"How long have they been married?" I said.

"Don't know," Bryan said. "But they've lived here about two years."

"I never noticed them move in," I said.

"Of course you didn't," Bryan said.

"I did," David said, looking at his beer.

Tina came home from work two hours later than usual. She'd called and said she would, told me she was going out to have a few drinks with some of the girls who worked at the Social Security office. I ordered pizza—the kids were excited about that. We left two slices for Tina, but when she came home, she said she'd had some food from the happy hour platter. She was also tipsy and started to act very affectionate, kissing me all over my face.

"You shouldn't drink and drive like that," I told her.

"Look who's talking," she said, touching the beer bottle I was holding. Then she grabbed it, and took a swig.

"I don't drink and drive," I told her.

"You've been drinking a lot lately."

"You've been spying on me," I laughed.

"I notice more things than you think, baby," she said, kissing me on the lips.

"You taste like tequila."

"Margaritas."

"How many'd you have?"

"You're sounding like a lawyer again," she said. "Three, counselor."

"With salt?"

"No."

"On the rocks?"

"Blended."

I asked, "So what did you and the girls talk about as you sat in some bar and drank margaritas?"

"I was the only one drinking margaritas," said Tina. "We started talking about work. Then we talked about men."

"Were there men in the bar?"

"Oh yes."

"Anyone try to pick you up?"

"I think I got a few looks."

"Smart men."

"I'm *horny*," she said.

She was reaching into my cut-off shorts. I touched her short blond hair, the tanned skin of her shoulders.

"Not in front of the kids!" I pleaded.

We went to the bedroom. It was a quick copulation. I was thinking about the sexy British woman in the short skirt and the screeching tires. I don't know what Tina was thinking about. She had her eyes closed and was louder than usual. The proper description would be vocally appreciative. I don't remember her ever having more than one or two drinks at a time. I suspected she'd had more than three margaritas tonight.

"God, I needed that," she said when we were done.

I imagined her saying that with a sultry British accent.

6

I was, in retrospect, obsessed with Cassandra Payne, more so in the beginning than I realized, or wanted to believe.

Had I known how sickening and utterly disturbed my behavior would eventually become, I would've stopped myself right then and there, and my life—everyone's lives—would be different today.

But you can't think that way, it'll only make you depressed and crazy.

You have to accept your actions and live with the consequences, as I do now.

I couldn't help myself; there was a wonderfully sexy, beautiful woman living across the street whose life, whose very existence, was a puzzle and a mystery.

Maybe I wasn't in love with my wife anymore. Maybe it was all a midlife crisis thing.

I began to take note of her comings and goings. She had no set schedule. Her husband, who drove a black BMW, usually left early—if he was around—or came home late. Sometimes the BMW would be there, but he'd depart or arrive by cab, with flight luggage. He was a tall, thin man, much like his wife, with silver-gray hair and thick glasses. He always wore three-piece suits.

When I was sitting around with either Bryan or David, we always stopped whatever we were talking about to observe the woman as she was leaving her house or coming home—and we took stock, of course, of what she was wearing. Cassandra Payne could make a potato sack sexy on her body. We never said anything about her, not usually, resuming whatever it was we were saying when she either left or went inside; but I could see it in their eyes, and Bryan and David probably saw it in mine: in our fantasies, we were undressing her, touching her, kissing her, making love to her. It didn't matter that Bryan and I were married, that she was an unattainable woman, a forbidden neighbor—in the world of fantasy, anything was possible and everything was permissible.

I continued with my home life, my married life, and became more and more curious about what went on inside the house across the street, and what went on inside Cassandra Payne's head.

In a dream I had of her, she came to me and offered me a berry. It was a red berry.

"Eat it," she said, "and we'll be married forever."

I had no idea what the dream meant.

My son, Matthew, was starting to have problems at school—he was getting into fights with other boys. He told me that the other boys started it, but his teacher said otherwise.

"Fighting does no good," I told my son. "People get hurt—people get arrested and file lawsuits over fights. People lose teeth, break bones."

"They're jerks," Matthew said.

"Who?"

"Everyone."

"How are they jerks?"

"They just are!" he huffed, and crossed his arms, and wouldn't look at me.

I was worried about him. He seemed to be getting more and more angry and destructive.

I told myself it was a phase for five-year-old boys. I recalled getting into some fights at his age . . . I think.

Jessica, I knew, would grow up to be a striking woman, perhaps as beautiful as Cassandra Payne. Men would adore her, chase her. She'd have no problem finding success in her future. It made me uncomfortable to think of my three-year-old daughter as a grown woman and using her sex appeal to make her way through the world.

Tina started going out with "the girls" one night a week, usually on Thursdays. She'd come home drunk, and she would either be frisky or she'd fall right to sleep. I thought it was good that she and her friends went out and blew off steam.

We were starting to get a lot of crank phone calls. At first, they were hang-ups, and then sounds, like gurgling, hissing, panting, gargling. I ordered Caller ID from the phone company; when it arrived in the mail, I immediately installed it. So when the next crank call came, and someone moaned and panted and hung up, I looked at the phone number on the little ID machine.

"Gotcha."

I dialed the number.

A kid's voice answered, male: "Hullo."

"Listen you little twerp," I said, "if you call here one more time, I will tell your parents, and I will go over to your house and open up a can of whup-ass and whup your ass, you hear?"

He hung up, I called him back.

"Uh, hullo?"

I panted and moaned. I really got into it, too.

He hung up.

I laughed.

Someone was pulling at my shirt. It was Jessica. She frowned and said, "Daddy, what are you doing?"

"Just playing," I said.

My daughter gave me a weird look. I was no better than the silly kid who'd been making the calls.

But the calls stopped.

One night, I had an idea. Tina and I were in bed. She was reading a book; I was lying next to her, looking at the ceiling.

"Let's have a party," I said.

"What?"

"A barbecue type deal, during the day," I said. "We'll cook food, invite our friends, even the neighbors." I sounded excited about this, too.

"Why?" she asked.

"Why not? When's the last time we had a get-together?"

"Before Jessica was born," she said.

"You see. Plus, it'd be a good way to acquaint ourselves with our neighbors."

"You *know* the neighbors."

"Just Bryan and David."

She thought about this, and nodded. "It'd be good to see some old friends, too."

"So let's do it," I said.

"You get it together and arrange it," she said.

"Deal," I said.

The master bedroom was on the bottom floor, the kids had their bedrooms upstairs, the third room outfitted as my office. I hadn't used it much since being disbarred, but the office had a new purpose: the window looked right across at the Paynes' home. Some nights, while Tina slept, I sat at my desk, the curtains drawn, and espied the house. I'd see shadows move about, hers and his. One time, their shadows confronted each other, and I could distantly hear them having an argument that only lasted a minute. Another time, her shadow swayed back and forth, like she was dancing. I wondered what kind of music she listened to.

7

We had the party two weeks later. I called friends, Tina called friends and told her coworkers. I printed up a few flyers and disbursed them throughout the neighborhood. I saved the Paynes' house for last. I was nervous and sweating. At last, I would see her up close; and I half-hoped she would reveal herself to be less striking face to face than from afar, then I could be released from this swelling fixation.

I waited approximately forty minutes after she got home. She was wearing white slacks and a suit jacket that day, her hair pulled up. I checked myself in the mirror several times. I was wearing a Hawaiian shirt and khaki slacks—I wanted to appear casual and festive.

The kids were playing with toys in front of the TV. They'd be all right. I hurried across the street.

My heart began to beat fast. I was acting like a teenage kid in heat and I thought this was just ridiculous.

I rang the doorbell. No answer.

I knocked on the door.

The door opened. I almost ran away. Cassandra Payne wasn't there, but her husband was. I didn't know he was home; his car was there, but that didn't mean anything. His arrival must've slipped by me, maybe while I was out passing flyers, or when I was in the bathroom.

"Yes?" he said. His tie was loose, he had dark circles under his eyes. I'd say he was in his late forties or early fifties, a lot of distinguished lines on his face.

"Hi, um hi," I said, holding out the flyer. He took it and arched a brow as he read. "I live across the street, I'm—"

He smiled. "Oh, yes, of course." He held out his hand. "Lawrence Payne."

"Philip Lansdale."

"You're having a bit of a shindig this weekend, I gather," he said with that refined British accent, referring to the flyer.

"Oh yes," I said. "Some close friends, and neighbors! What better way to get to know the people who live around you, don't you think?"

"Yes, that's not my strongest point," he said. "I'm out of town a lot, as my work calls for it."

I wanted to say, *I know.*

"I'm sure my wife Cassy and I can drop in. Have you met my wife?"

"Well," I said, "no."

"She's in the bath right now. Always takes these awful long baths and never wants to be disturbed. But when she comes out, I'll tell her about this," he said, holding up the flyer.

"Thanks."

"Thank you for thinking of us," Payne said. "Perhaps we will see you this weekend."

"Perhaps," I said, "that'd be nice." I felt stupid.

He smiled, I smiled, we shook hands, he closed the door, and I walked across the street and back to my house. All I could think about was the man's wife in a bathtub, bubbles and water all around her clean white body, her hands touching herself.

Her husband was in love with her, I could tell; he adored her and I'm sure she adored him back. I was married, too. These thoughts, these desires—I *was* an idiot. I had too much time on my hands, that was the problem.

I opened a beer when I got home, but what I really wanted was some of Bryan's vodka.

I didn't expect such a good turnout. Fortunately, Tina persuaded me to prepare for such an eventuality—"People just don't easily turn down free food and booze, and no one does anything on Sundays except go to church and lay around the house," she said.

People started arriving after one in the afternoon; by three, there were at least forty people mingling about my backyard and in the rooms of my house. My children were confused and delighted by all these guests. I think Tina was surprised by the number; we were both very busy hosts. Bryan and his demure and elegant wife, Ellen, the librarian, took it upon themselves to man the portable barbecue, cooking up hot dogs, hamburgers, and small steaks. Bryan, always with a drink in hand, was wearing a chef's hat and apron, and he was having a grand old time cooking away; Ellen attended to the condiments. David, much to my surprise, showed up with a date—or, at least a woman at his side, and a very young woman at that, I'd say not too many days over eighteen, and (he confessed) a student of his.

It was nice to see some of the old friends and acquaintances Tina and I had acquired over the years, either through my job or hers, or through mutual friends. I met some of Tina's co-workers, who seemed pleased (and curious) to meet me—the husband.

I put on music—classic songs from the seventies and eighties—and people began to dance, after they drank more. I had plenty of alcohol on hand: refrigerator and two ice chests full of beer, a well-stocked supply of gin, tequila, vodka, bourbon, and whiskey.

Around five-thirty, Cassandra Payne showed up. She was alone.

She was wearing a long charcoal gray skirt with slits on each side, slits that went high, revealing the pale flesh of her naked skin; the skirt was so tight that you could make out the outline of her underwear, the v-shape of the thong riding between the cheeks of her ass. She also wore black leather boots that came up to the tip of her calves, and a blue suit jacket unbuttoned enough to show her white chest and part of a gray bra. Gold necklace, gold earrings, no rings on her fingers. Her fragrance was gentle but bespoke expensive designer perfume. She wore little makeup, just a touch of lipstick and eyeliner. She knew she was the center of attention at that moment, and you could tell she liked it, she was used to it, perhaps she even expected and thrived on it.

I approached her, Tina trailing behind me.

"Philip Lansdale," I said, smiling, and heard my wife softly cough. "And this is Tina, Tina Lansdale—we're your, ah, hosts."

"Yes," she said with her thick British accent, which was even more smooth and stylized than her husband's. "Yes, of course," shaking Tina's hand first, and then mine, and looking me in the eye. "Cassandra Payne, your neighbor across the street." Her eyebrows were unusually thick and dark, and almost met; her chin chiseled and defined. There was something masculine about her face, but this didn't detract from her inherent beauty . . . it was a curiosity. She was quite tall, almost as tall as me with those boots, and extremely thin—all these attributes that I knew well, seeing her from afar, were more evident close-up.

"Glad you could make it," Tina said flatly.

"Will your husband be joining us?" I asked. "Lawrence. I talked to him the other day."

"I'm afraid not," she said. "He was called out on unexpected business. I didn't want to be rude, I wanted to come by and say hello."

"Well," Tina said, "I hope you'll be staying longer than just a hello."

"Yes," was Cassandra Payne's reply.

"Would you like a drink?" I said. "A beer?"

Very slightly, she turned up her nose at the mention of

beer—other people may not have noticed such a subtle motion, but I—having observed people during depositions and trials—noticed.

"A bourbon on the rocks would be most pleasant," she said.

"Coming right up," I was too eager, I know, but I went to the table where the alcohol was and poured two shots of Jim Beam in a cup, adding ice. Cassandra Payne stood where I left her, looking around, as people continued to mingle and talk, while watching her out of the corner of their eyes. Especially David—he acted like he was having a conversation with his date, but his attention was really on the British woman.

I saw her smile at him, and David quickly looked away.

I returned and gave her the cup.

"Thank you." She sipped at the bourbon.

"Food's out in the backyard," I said. "Your other neighbor, Bryan Vaughn, piloting the barbecue. Have you ever had barbecue?" I asked, and immediately wished I could retract that question.

She seemed to think about it, though. "I believe I have. Steak. Well-done."

"Ahhhh," I said, nodding, not knowing what else to say, wanting to rip open her jacket and see the size of her breasts. "I just meant—you being English—" I didn't know what I meant.

"Perhaps," she said, with a smile, "a bite to eat would prove prudent. I haven't eaten all day."

"Yeah, well, help yourself to all the grub you want."

She walked toward the back of the house, to the yard. I wished I hadn't said "grub."

Tina was standing next to me. "Where did she come from? Out of a fashion magazine or a bad TV show?"

"What?"

"A bourbon on the rocks would be most pleasant," Tina mimicked a British accent, very low. " 'A bite to eat would prove prudent.' "

"Are you making fun of her?"

"Watch your eyes, Philip," hitting me on the arm.

"What?" I laughed it off.

"You can't help it, I know. And every other man here has bug-eyes." Walking away, she added, "But I don't know if she's really a woman, you know . . ."

I waited until Tina was talking to a friend, and went to the backyard. Cassandra Payne was in conversation with Bryan and Ellen. They laughed about something. Bryan handed Ellen a hot dog, which she put in a bun and added mayonnaise and mustard, and with a napkin, passed it along to Mrs. Payne.

I watched her eat the hot dog, holding a cup of bourbon like Matthew had while looking at the flames flickering from the trash can.

"Philip."

I jumped. It was Ray McCann, a lawyer I was acquainted with. He was quickly balding, in his early thirties, and it seemed, right now, like he was well on the way to a good drunk.

"Hey," I said.

He was nodding at her. "Who's the babe?"

"My neighbor."

"Do say! Will you introduce me? Does she like lawyers? Would she go out with a lawyer?"

"She's married."

"So are most women you meet," he said. "What does it matter?" He waited, then said, "Introduce me."

"Introduce yourself, Ray," I said. "Be bold. Be aggressive. Shouldn't be hard for an *attorney*."

"Right," he said, straightening what little hair he had. He made his way to her, or weaved. She looked at him. He turned and walked in a different direction. She was looking at me now. I smiled. She smiled. She approached me, a subtle swing in her hips.

"I should be going," she said. "I have an appointment."

I wanted to ask what the appointment was, and who with. I almost did, then my daughter joined us.

"Hello," my daughter said.

"Well, hello there, little girl." Cassandra Payne bent down to touch my daughter's shoulder. I was surprised she could make the move in her tight skirt, but the slits helped, and exposed a lot of leg. I could see down her jacket. I could see more skin. I think I was shaking. "What's your name?" she asked my daughter.

"Jessica."

"Jessica. That's a nice name."

My daughter was holding a plastic dinosaur and she said, "This is Bobby."

"Bobby the Brontosaurus?"

"Just Bobby," Jessica said.

"You're very pretty, little Jessica," Cassandra Payne said. "So is Bobby."

"You're very pretty, lady," Jessica said.

David was watching all this, from afar. So was Tina.

Cassandra Payne stood. "This is your girl?" she asked me. "Yeah."

"I've seen her about. She's a charmer."

"She speaks the truth," I said.

Cassandra Payne didn't register that, or acted as if she didn't. "Well," she said, "thank you for the booze and hot dog."

"It's very American," I said. Boy, I was just full of dumb remarks. "Booze and hot dogs, I mean."

"Crackerjacks, hot dogs, beer, apple pie, and baseball," she said, holding out her hand. We shook hands, and then she left. I wanted to hold on to that warm, moist, feminine hand for hours.

Her smell lingered, or so I thought.

Her exit was as noteworthy as her entrance.

From the window, I watched her get into her Taurus and drive away.

The party went on.

Toward sundown, only the hard-core drunks were left. I was sitting with Ray McCann. I was drinking Jim Beam on the rocks.

"My practice is growing well," he said, slurring every word.

"That's good."

"Why don't you come work for me, Philip?"

"You know I've been disbarred," I said. "Something I should be ashamed of but I'm too shitfaced and stuffed with hot dogs to care right now."

"You could work as a paralegal."

I gave him a look.

"Or maybe as an investigator."

"I think my days in the legal world are over," I said, and suddenly felt depressed. This could very well be true. All the years I spent in law school, working in the system, and here I was, a drunk house husband with infidelity on his mind.

"What will you do?"

"Do I need to do anything?"

"You're okay?"

"I'm okay," I smiled. "Thanks. Really."

"Well, if you change your mind . . ."

"I'll be right at your door," I said.

I wondered, when he was sober, if he'd really give me a job.

8

Two days later, Cassandra Payne had a visitor. That would make it Tuesday. From this point, each day, each hour, becomes important, because it gives me a road map to what happened to my life from the day of the party until now.

Bryan, David, and I were doing our usual thing, sitting around in white lawn chairs, drinking beer, and talking. A small sports car—a Datsun 280Z—shiny red with a loud engine—stopped in front of the Paynes' house. A very thin man got out. He wore jeans, a black T-shirt, and a black leather jacket. He also had shades on—Raybans. He walked with a bounce. His long hair was in a ponytail and he had a goatee. He knocked on the door. Cassandra Payne answered. I couldn't catch what she was wearing, the man was in the way, but I believe she may have been wearing a robe. She hugged the man. They lightly kissed on the lips.

This is what I was thinking: *She has a lover?*

From the looks on Bryan and David's faces, they were wondering the same.

The man went inside, and the door closed.

"Well, well," Bryan said.

"She's never had company before," David noted. "I don't think. Has she?"

"Nope," Bryan said.

No, I thought.

"I wonder who he is," David said.

"Who do you think he is?" Bryan asked.

"He could be anybody."

"He's somebody."

I said, "Her squeeze?"

"Bingo," Bryan said.

"Do you think she's the kind to cheat on her husband?" David asked.

Bryan said, "I think she's the kind that just might do about *any*thing."

"No," I said.

"What?"

"He could be an old friend."

"He could be her brother," David said.

"He could be that," I said.

"Or someone who fucks better than Mr. Payne," Bryan laughed.

David said, "If that's so, where did she meet him? At a bar? At a club?"

"At the park?" I added.

"At work," Bryan said.

"We don't know if she works," I said.

"Well she does *some*thing," Bryan said, "all that in and out."

David laughed. Bryan laughed. I joined, but it was fake. I was jealous. That man might be making love to her right now, kissing her . . . *in and out* . . .

"Maybe he's a drug dealer," I said, "dropping off an order."

Bryan raised his eyebrows. "Now there's something."

"He kind of looks like a drug dealer."

"Yes, he does."

"Our Cassandra," David said, "a drug user?"

"You bet," Bryan said.

"What kind of drugs, you think? Pot?"

"Coke or meth," Bryan said.

"Or heroin."

Bryan said, "If he is a dealer, he won't stay long. Drop off the package, get his money, and go."

"Unless he screws her, too," David said.

"Good point."

The visitor didn't come out soon, or at all. An hour went

by. Everything was quiet and uneventful across the street. David went home. Ellen drove up, and Bryan went home. Tina drove up, and we both went inside. I made dinner and Tina and I put the kids to bed. As Tina was taking a shower, I went outside. The sports car was still there. There were no lights on in the Payne house. They were fucking in the dark, I just knew it. I wanted to go over there and look in the window and verify my fear. I wanted to pound on the door and stop them. I wanted to call her on the phone and say, "What would your husband think if he knew?"

I didn't have her phone number.

Later, I woke up from the sound of a car starting. I looked at the clock: 2:45 A.M. Tina was lightly snoring next to me. I slipped out of bed, wearing boxers, and peeked out the window. The sports car was driving away. Cassandra Payne stood on the porch, the features of her face shadowed by the dim porch light, her hair messy. She wore a dark robe that she clutched around her. She was staring at the car, watching it go down the street and turn the corner. She did not have the look of a woman who'd just been in the throes of passion and was sad to see her lover depart. She looked worried

Maybe it was a trick of the shadows.

9

Thursday night, two days later, the police converged on our neighborhood. There were two squad cars and two unmarked Oldsmobile sedans. They were at the Paynes' house.

Tina was out with her girlfriends, Thursday being her going-out-and-drinking night. The kids were asleep. The cops didn't arrive with sirens, but I could hear the commotion of their radios—dispatchers, other cars calling in. I went outside. I feared something bad had happened to Cassandra Payne. Bryan and Ellen came out of their house and looked, as did everyone else in the neighborhood.

"Do you think something happened to her?" I asked Bryan. He shrugged.

"Maybe she called them," Ellen said. "Maybe there was a prowler."

Bryan said, "I'm gonna go over there and find out."

"Can you do that?" Ellen said.

"I used to be a cop, dear." He smiled.

" 'Used to be,' " his wife said. She didn't smile back.

"I'm also a concerned citizen," he said. With that, he hoisted up his shorts and marched across the street. He talked to a uniformed officer at the door. The officer said something over his shoulder, then nodded, and let Bryan in. Ellen and I looked at each other. The minutes went by very slowly. Ellen and I looked at each other again.

"Tina isn't home yet," I said, because I didn't know what else to say.

Ellen nodded. She was worried.

A news van drove up. The logo on the van's side was the local station KUSI. One of the uniformed cops talked to the news people; it seemed like the cop was trying to get them to leave. Another news van arrived, and then another.

Five minutes later, Bryan came out of the house, shaking his head.

"What is it?" Ellen said.

"It's her husband, Lawrence," Bryan said. "There's a homicide detective in there, Roger. I know him."

"What about her husband?" I said.

"Apparently, he's been murdered."

Ellen drew in a breath, touching her chest. "Bryan, my God."

"Killed in a taxicab coming from the airport," he said. "Cab driver's dead, too. Bullet wounds."

Tina's car pulled up in the driveway. She got out, her eyes glazed with booze.

"Our neighbor's been murdered," I told her.

"The British woman?" Tina said.

"Her husband," Ellen said.

"Oh," my wife said. "*Oh . . .*"

Bryan said, "They just came to tell her. And ask if she knew anyone who might want him dead. But from what I've been told, it sounds like a drive-by shooting. Maybe random. A gang thing."

"Was she crying?" I heard myself say. "Cassandra Payne?"

"No," Bryan said.

"Philip," Tina said, "what kind of question is that?"

I didn't respond.

Ellen said, "Bryan, let's go inside. There's nothing to accomplish out here."

Bryan nodded. He looked different, maybe like the cop he used to be—here was a crime, and his mind was working on how to solve it.

"Poor woman," Ellen said as she and Bryan walked away.

———

"**I couldn't face** living day after day if you died," Tina said when we went inside our house. She made herself a screwdriver, and I had one too. We sat at the dining room table and drank. The cops were still across the street. "Especially if you were murdered. I just couldn't go on," she said.

"What would you do?"

"I don't know."

"And the kids?"

"I'd have to raise them alone," she said. "But life would be a living hell." She reached out to touch my hand.

"It would be for me too," I said softly. "If you were gone."

"I don't plan to be. Do you?"

"No."

"That poor woman," she said, sounding like Ellen.

"Yeah."

"I don't even want to think about what she must be going through."

It was in the newspapers the next morning, and on the TV: the shooting death of Lawrence Payne, and a taxicab driver. "Investment banker Lawrence Payne was found murdered in a cab last night, along with a cab driver, Darron Gregory," the anchorwoman on TV said. "Payne, a citizen of the United Kingdom and a vice president at the Consolidated Bank of Manchester on Second and Ash, had returned from a business trip and taken a cab from Lindbergh Field. The taxi was found on First and Grape. Both Payne and the driver were shot. At this time, police have not reported any motive or suspects. Lawrence Payne is survived by his wife, also a British national, living in San Diego's North Park area."

Tina thought about not going to work. I told her that was ridiculous. This was not our tragedy.

"It just makes me think what a scary world it is out there," she said.

I kissed her on the forehead. "I'll protect you from the scary world."

"Always?"

"Always."

"And the kids?"

"Always," I said.

She went to work, and I drove Matthew to school, Jessica in the back playing with her assortment of plastic dinosaurs and Pokémon.

Most of the day, I kept an eye on the Payne house. Bryan didn't join me. He wasn't home. I didn't know where he was.

Cassandra Payne. She had two visitors, both cops.

Later in the afternoon, David came over with a six-pack of Budweiser.

"Where's Bryan?" he said, handing me a beer.

I said I didn't know.

"Some excitement last night, I hear." He seemed nervous.

"Where were you?"

"I went to see a play," he blurted.

"A play!" I said.

"Hey, culture," he said, shrugging.

"I didn't know there was any culture in San Diego," I said.

"You have to search hard to find it," David said, looking away.

"So I guess you know everything."

"Jesus," he said after a while. "Murdered."

"Yeah," I said, opening a second beer.

"You think someone had it in for him?"

"Bryan thinks it was a gang."

"A gang wanted him?"

"Random shooting. An initiation."

"I've heard about that stuff," he said. "Like the Crips—you either have to cripple or murder someone to get in the gang."

"Don't believe everything you hear and see on TV," I said.

"I read it in a very respectable magazine," he told me. "These things happen, Philip. It's a different world out there."

I wanted to ask: *Out where?*

The phone rang a little after midnight. I wasn't asleep. I was in my office, looking out the window, searching for any signs of my neighbor: the new widow.

I quickly picked up the extension on the second ring. I was expecting bad news at this hour.

"Philip."

"Bryan?"

"Sorry to call so late."

"What's wrong?"

"Meet me outside," he said. "We need to talk."

I went downstairs and checked on Tina. She was on her back, eyes closed; the phone hadn't woken her. I went out the backyard, around the side gate, and met Bryan between our properties. He was wearing a leather jacket with his pajamas and slippers and holding a bottle of vodka. He looked comic. His expression was serious.

He held the vodka bottle out. It was Absolut Citrön. "Ah, the good stuff," I said, and took a swig.

"We need to keep our voices down," he whispered. "Don't wanna wake up the whole neighborhood." He glanced across the street and sighed.

"Okay," I whispered back. "What is it?"

"You've been paying close attention to her, right?"

"Who?"

He turned to me. "Don't play dumb. It's on your face every time you see her—you're undressing her and fucking her every chance you get. If I was twenty years younger, I would be, too. And it's not like I haven't entertained the notion of a roll in the hay with the woman myself. You notice when she comes and goes because you like to watch her."

Damn ex-cop. "Yeah."

"How many times did she leave yesterday?"

"Once."

"What time?"

"Around," I had to think, "three."

"So she was home all day?"

"Yeah."

"But she usually leaves more than once a day."

"Usually."

"What time did she come back?"

"Six-thirty," I said.

"So she was gone for three and a half hours."

"Bryan—"

"Lawrence Payne's flight came in from New York at five-fifteen. The taxi driver reported to his dispatcher that he was leaving the airport terminal at five-thirty-five, going to North Park. The taxi with Payne and the driver was discovered at nine o'clock. They weren't but a few minutes outside the airport. Sometime before six is when the murder took place. Probably, say, five-forty-five. Mrs. Payne comes home at six-thirty. It's a fifteen minute drive from the airport to here. Twenty, tops."

"Jesus, Bryan, what are you getting at?" But I already knew. I took a swig from the vodka bottle.

He said, "I spent the day hanging out at the substation. Trying to glean information, you know. I was also a little useful, being a neighbor. But I really don't know squat. What I *do* know is she told the investigating officers that she was home all day."

"What?"

"Yep. Said she never set foot out the door."

"But—"

"But we know she did, from three to six-thirty."

"Did you tell the cops this?"

"I just found this information out," he said, "from you."

"I see," I said. "Will you tell the cops?"

"Not yet. She may change her story. Maybe she was so upset that she forgot she went out to get her nails done. Didn't think it was significant. Maybe you got your days mixed up."

"No. I don't have my—"

"I didn't think so."

"What are you saying, Bryan?"

He drank. "You know what I'm saying."

"No," I said, "I do not." I did.

"Our little lady over there may very well be a murderess."

I tried to make light of this. "Come on Bryan, you're *not* serious."

"You forget I worked homicide. I can smell a killer, and I think I smell one."

"Why would she kill her husband?" I said.

"Why does any person kill a spouse? It happens every day for very common reasons: jealousy, fear, greed. In this case, I believe it may be greed. Lawrence Payne was a banker, he made good money, he may have had *access* to a lot of money. And he's twice her age. Did you know that?"

"Well, he doesn't seem older—"

"We were thinking, what? That Mrs. Payne was in her late twenties, early thirties?"

"Yeah."

"She's twenty-three."

"Oh," I said.

"And he's forty-eight."

"It's not that uncommon."

"No. But it's fishy, wouldn't you say? She said she was married to him for four years. That means she was nineteen when she hitched up with the guy."

I said, "So you think she left the house, knowing he was taking a cab home, and somehow shot him? How?"

"Pulls up alongside the cab. Payne recognizes his wife, he says, 'Good Heavens, that's my wife,' " Bryan said in a funny British accent, "and the cab pulls over, and she pulls out the gun, and—bang bang."

"Oh boy," I said.

"But I really don't think that's the way it happened." He took a swig of vodka. "Two days before the murder, she had a visitor, as you will no doubt recall."

"Yes," I said.

"Who stayed most of the night."

I nodded.

"Perhaps a lover. Most *likely* a lover."

"Maybe," I said. "Or a friend."

"A shifty-looking fellow," Bryan said, "maybe a *killer*."

"Bryan . . ."

"Think about it. He was young. He's her lover. The husband has money. She wants the lover, not the husband. The lover wants the girl *and* the money. So he kills the husband. She's in on it. They planned it: she told him when his flight was coming in. The lover's at the airport, sees Payne get into a cab. The lover follows the cab, waits until they're at a dark intersection—which is just where the cab was—pulls alongside the cab in that nifty little sports car he was driving, and bang bang," he pointed a gun-finger for emphasis this time, aiming at the Payne house.

"But why kill the driver?"

"He was there. Don't leave a witness."

"You didn't forward these theories to your friends in the police department?" I asked, feeling like a lawyer again.

"No, not yet. I kept quiet. And I'm going to keep quiet for the time being."

"Like, for instance, that she did indeed leave yesterday when she said she hadn't?"

"Right."

"And that she had this visitor . . ."

"You got it."

"And that we could be barking up a wrong tree here," I said.

He sighed. "That too. So this is what I propose: you and I will keep an eye on her."

"The two of us?"

"We'll just watch what she does in the next few days. People who've committed murder—or are accessories to such—will do certain telling things over the first few days after the crime, things that they'd normally never do, things they will try to do in secret, *but* if someone were watching them . . ."

"Their actions may reveal their guilt," I said.

He smiled. "You're getting the picture, kid. I knew I liked you for some reason."

"And I suppose we start tonight."

"Tonight is a good night."

I asked, "What about tomorrow's game?"

"We can't miss a game," Bryan said. "One of us needs to hurry back. No. I got a better idea. You'll call in sick. You can't play."

"I like playing," and that sounded funny coming out of me, like a child talking to his father.

"I know you like the game, son, but you need to keep watch. You like watching her anyway."

I felt uncomfortable. "This could all be for nothing," I said.

He winked and said, "Have anything better to do?"

10

I played hooky from the baseball game. I had to act sick for Tina and the kids. I feigned a stomachache.

"I must've ate something bad," I groaned.

"It's all the booze you've been consuming," Tina said, gently rubbing my belly. "You're starting to get a gut, too, *dude*."

"A gut?" I looked down. She was right. "I should do some sit-ups," I said.

"Wouldn't hurt."

Part of the ruse was staying in bed, which wasn't so bad. I watched TV. I kept the window open, so I could hear whether or not my neighbor left her house.

She didn't. Not once all day. I spotted her getting the mail around three, wearing jeans and a T-shirt, her hair pulled into a ponytail. I'd never seen her appear so—plain and ordinary, like any other person at home on a Saturday.

I tried meditating on the joy of family life; I knew the joy was there, I just couldn't get a grasp on it. I realized I wasn't happy. I was happy with my life when I was busy with work, and now that I was busy with home life, I needed something else.

I thought about these issues all that day, and long into the night, as I sat in my office, in the dark, drinking straight from a bottle of Smirnoff, watching. I was halfway through the bottle and feeling pretty buzzed, going through my years, month by month, before I met Tina and married—cataloging the good times and the bad, past loves and conquests, trying to remember, exactly, how all their bodies felt, how they smelled, how they fucked.

I wondered if Tina gave any thought to these recent late hours I'd been spending in my office? Did she notice I was missing from the bed? She never stirred when I did go to bed.

She was oblivious to me—she slept heavily, which was either to my advantage or part of my downfall.

At five minutes past 1 A.M., a light went on inside the Paynes' house.

Three minutes later, the sports car and the mysterious visitor arrived. She knew he was coming—had it been preplanned? "Come by at one-ten." Or had he called first, perhaps on a cell phone or from a phone booth?

He seemed in a rush, jumping out of his car. She opened the door to let him in. I couldn't see how she was dressed. He was dressed the same as the other day.

He didn't stay long. I could faintly see their shadowed silhouettes—they were talking. Arms were gesturing wildly. I cracked the window open. I was sure I could hear them arguing. Then the door flew open, and he stormed out, yelling, "Fuck you!"

"Keep your voice down," she said.

"Fuck you!" he said, and got into his car. He had an American accent, southwest I'd say.

"Fuck you too," she replied softly.

I wrote down his license plate—hoping I got it right, straining my eyes and trying to read the numbers. Nevada plates.

He drove off, burning rubber.

I wondered if Bryan heard the commotion.

She was wearing the same robe, and it was open. I could see her white chest, the beginning contours of her small breasts. She closed the door. The light turned off.

I saw a light come on, faintly, at the side of the house. Bedroom light, I wondered?

I sat there and drank.

It was so quiet. I could hear every creak in the house.

I heard music coming from her house.

It was almost two o'clock. I was at the bottom of the bottle. I was feeling bold. She had turned the music up—it was soft jazz. Sexy. The music of fuck.

I had a crazy idea and I was just drunk enough to do it. A lot of Smirnoff in your blood makes you very bold, and stupid.

I went outside and stalked across the street. The neighborhood was dark and dead—porch lights, a few cats walking around, a slight breeze, half a moon in the night sky. I stood on her property. I crept like a prowler, aware of every piece of grass, dirt, and leaf I trespassed on. I saw the window where the light and music were coming from. I pressed my back against the side of the house and slid to the window. It was in fact the bedroom window, and what I saw, well, I wasn't expecting—I may have fantasized about it, but I didn't think I'd ever see this in the flesh—

I should say *her* in the flesh—

Cassandra Payne was dancing slowly to the music, solitaire, glass of dark liquid in her thin hand. Her robe was loosening, one shoulder bare. She hummed to herself, either simulating the notes of the music, or making up words, I couldn't tell. She sipped from the glass and swayed. She looked content. This didn't seem right for a woman who'd just lost her husband two days ago. It could've been a British thing for all I knew.

She stopped in front of the full-length mirror on the wall. She looked at herself. She was licking her lips, eyeing her body up and down. I could make out my own face in the mirror, in the background, peering in the window. For a moment, I was afraid she might see this reflection—and then I realized I didn't care. Being caught while beholding this phenomenal display would be worth it.

She began to make love to herself.

She drank most of what was left of the brown liquid, coughing once. She dropped the glass on the carpet. Her robe slipped down. She stood completely naked in front of the mirror, except for her gray socks. She started at her neck: touching this long, pale neck lightly with her fingernails. She moved from the neck down to her chest and breasts. She masturbated slowly, and then gradually brought herself to a frenzy; flesh quivering, moaning—

I was ashamed and frightened. What was I doing here? I didn't stay and watch her. I could have, she didn't seem anywhere close to stopping. I quickly ran back to my house, my home, the safety of that darkness. I felt dirty. I had glimpsed something I should not have—I had seen a person in an intense, private moment. It was if I had spied on God creating life and now I was doomed to the netherworld of loneliness.

I wasn't drunk anymore, either. The moment had sobered me up.

I didn't fall asleep until four-thirty. It was restless, erotic sleep, Cassandra Payne haunting my dreams—I was following her all over San Diego like a private investigator, and everywhere she went, she masturbated—in restaurants, libraries, parks, and movie theaters.

I told Bryan about her nighttime visitor. I didn't tell him about what I saw in the window. I gave him the license plate number. He smiled and said, "Good boy. I'll call in a favor and see if we can't get an ident on Mr. Mystery Man."

"Good idea," I said.

"Something is fishy in Great Britain," Bryan added, and winked.

"Indeed," I said.

She didn't leave or have any visitors all Sunday.

Bryan came over Monday, around noon. He had a six-pack of Amstel. He gave me one, opened one for himself. Cassandra Payne was inside her house.

"His name is Boyd Urick," he said.

I almost asked who. I said, "Wait. I may have gotten the numbers wrong—"

"No, this is the right man. Nevada plates?"

"Right."

"And the description matches."

"So you called in the favor."

"It wasn't a problem," Bryan said. "He's twenty-seven years old, was born in Pahrump, Nevada."

"Where the hell is that?"

"Small town in Nye County, maybe sixty miles away from Las Vegas. That's where Mr. Urick lives: Las Vegas. Occupation unknown. I'd say he's either a blackjack dealer or a card-player—as in professional gambler."

"Or with the mob."

"Maybe. His rap sheet fits the profile. His arrests and convictions were misdemeanors—petty theft, driving with an expired license—and a felony, writing bad checks. There were some other felony charges of grand theft and forgery that didn't stick. I'd say a good candidate for a killer."

"They were arguing about something," I said. "They argued like they'd done it before, like they knew each other."

"They probably do know each other."

"How?"

He shrugged, drank his beer. "I tried to get some information about Mrs. Payne from the homicide cop, Roger. He either wouldn't tell me or they don't have a history on her. I'd say they know nothing about her. She very well may have no history in the computers—married her husband back in jolly old England and came here."

"She had him killed," I said.

"Oh yeah," he said.

"Do we tell the cops now?"

"Not yet," he said. "Let's see what else happens. If Mr. Urick shows up again. If Mrs. Payne tries to disappear into the night." He was enjoying this, the game of sleuthing—he was a cop again. I liked seeing him this way, it made me feel good.

"Look," he said.

Cassandra Payne came out, wearing perhaps the shortest black leather miniskirt I had ever seen, and a white blouse. Her high heels clacked. Bryan and I stood there looking at her, both our jaws agape. She noticed us and waved. We waved back. She got into her Taurus and drove off.

"Maybe we should follow her," I suggested.

"Too obvious," Bryan said. "And I don't think we'd catch up to her even if we hopped into one of our cars right now. But you have to wonder, where is she going dressed like that? Those aren't clothes for mourning."

"Speaking of which," I said, "do you know if there's going to be a funeral?"

"Not sure. The ME may still have the body for evidence."

There'd been nothing else in the news about Lawrence Payne and the cab driver—the story was interesting for two minutes, now it was forgotten.

"Those legs," Bryan whistled. "That girl has some long fine legs on her, wouldn't you say?" He laughed.

"Yeah," I said, seeing her legs bent, her legs spread open, her hand at her crotch . . .

"*Killer* legs!" Bryan laughed.

I didn't find that funny.

Late at night, my family asleep, I watched.

Sitting in my office, the window open, drinking shots of Jim Beam, I waited for a sign. I wanted to know what she was drinking Saturday night. Was it bourbon? I wanted to believe so.

Certain kinds of hard alcohol put me in different moods. Vodka, it's an intellectual drunk. Tequila, I want to dance.

Scotch and bourbon, I want to fight—I feel like a true redneck, dumb enough to try and take on the world. Or fuck. Fight and fuck.

Needless to say, as the bourbon took hold of my senses, I was feeling invincible again, and I wanted another look into the private life of the woman, the killer.

It was almost 2 A.M.. and that light at the side of the house was on again—the bedroom light. I didn't hear music. I knew she was awake, I knew she was doing something that would be a treat for my eyes. I could replay every moment of her from Saturday night. I needed to do it again. So, again, I quietly slipped out of my house and went to hers.

I wasn't being as cautious this time, walking over. The boldness of booze. I didn't hear any music. I was hoping she'd be dancing again, that she'd play with herself for me. I looked in the window. She wasn't there. The light was on, but no sign of her. Maybe she was in the bathroom. I could wait. I would wait. I did wait. I waited five minutes and she still didn't come into the bedroom. There was no other light on in the house, as far as I could tell.

"Turn around, you."

I almost screamed. Her accent, cold and close—behind me.

"Turn around slowly."

I did. She stood there, in her robe, holding a kitchen knife. How had she crept up on me so quietly, so quickly?

"*You,*" she said, like she was surprised—or disappointed.

I felt like I was going to piss in my pants.

"You," she said again. "You *fucking* peeping Tom."

"I can explain," I said.

She smiled, lowering the knife. "I bet you can. Come inside and explain." She held up the knife. "Or else I'll slice your throat open." I didn't know if she was serious, but I followed her inside, going first. She was pointing the knife at my back.

A single candle lit the living room. The candle was on the

table, next to a bottle of Wild Turkey and a glass. It was the same glass she had Saturday night, or a similar glass. It was empty.

"Would you like a drink?" she asked.

"Yes, I would," I said.

She poured the glass half-full with Wild Turkey and handed it to me. I drank. She took the bottle and drank, knife still in one hand, eyeing me. She sat down on a couch and told me to sit on the couch across from her. I did. The flickering candle made flickering shadows on the walls and the floor.

"So, neighbor," she said. "Mr. Lansdale . . . you were peeking in my bedroom window."

I finished the bourbon; it burned in my blood and took some of the fear and shame away. "Yes," I said, "I was."

"What were you hoping to see?"

"What I saw Saturday night."

Her smile went away, and there was anger in her eyes. "That was *you* Saturday night?"

"What?"

"I knew I was being watched," she said. "I thought it was someone else. I thought it was . . ." She shook her head.

"Your boyfriend from Nevada?" I said.

Her smile returned; it wasn't an amused expression this time. "You've been keeping tabs on me. I know you have. You and the retired cop across the street. You think I don't know? A woman knows when she is being watched by the eyes of men. Your eyes send out signals. Does your *wife* know you watch me?"

I didn't respond to that.

"She doesn't know you're here. Hold out your glass, Mr. Lansdale."

I did. She reached over and poured more bourbon. Her robe opened; one pert, pink breast popped out. She sat back and didn't bother to pull the robe in. She drank from the bottle. I realized she was probably just as drunk and out of it as I was. Her legs were slightly parted. I noticed she was wearing dark nylons.

"Have you always been a voyeur, Mr. Lansdale?" she asked me.

"Did you kill your husband, Mrs. Payne?"

She laughed at that, loudly and hysterically. She shook the hair on her head, and drank. I drank. She stopped laughing.

"Is this what this is all about?" she said.

I said, "I don't know what anything is all about," and I drank. I wanted to drink myself into oblivion.

Silence. The candle flickered.

Cassandra Payne slid down a few inches, watching me. She dropped the knife to the floor. "Did you like what you saw the other night? Did you like watching me frig myself?" Her legs opened a little more. "I like to be watched, even if I didn't know it was you watching. But what does that matter now? Like they say: 'At this point, it's all water under the butt.' I mean *bridge*. Who are they anyway?" She drank. "Did you like watching me play with my pussy? *Answer* me, damn you, you pervert, you filthy peeping Tom, tell me, did you like it?"

"You're beautiful," I said. "You're the most beautiful woman I've ever seen."

She said, weakly, "You don't know anything, Mr. Lansdale. You're drunk."

"I mean it," I said. "I've been lusting for you—"

"For *how* long? Since I moved to this godforsaken quiet little patch of American suburbia?"

"Several weeks now."

"Adultery is a sin, even in the heart," she cackled.

I gulped down the rest of the booze. My head was spinning and I had to urinate badly.

"Come here and eat me," she said. "Don't think about it, just get your mouth over here into my crotch."

I didn't think about it, I didn't hesitate. I went to her. She grabbed my head with both hands and forced me closer, deeper, into her. I could feel the Wild Turkey bottle next to my ear. She guided the movement of my head, grabbing my ears and hair—first up and down, then back and forth, then pulling me in so hard that I thought I wasn't going to be able to breathe. Her pelvis buckled under me, and she came with a long grunt, and came again with a scream, and still she made me stay down there, her hands never leaving my head. I told her I wanted to fuck her. "You're not going to screw me, Mr. Lansdale," she hissed, "you don't deserve to; bad boys like you don't get to have any pleasure." If I tried to get free, I was afraid she'd hurt me, leave scratches. How would I explain that to Tina? I couldn't think of Tina at a time like this. Cassandra sighed, and then a gush of warm, salty fluid filled my mouth, splashed across my face and into my hair. She let go of me and I fell back, urine in my mouth. Her fluid spurt into the air and arced, like a fountain. I stood. I felt really stupid, and embarrassed, standing there.

Cassandra lay still on the couch. "Go away now," she said.

I no longer wanted her. I wanted to get the hell out of there, and I did.

I wanted to run, but I walked stiffly, entering my house from back. In the garage, I got out of my jeans and hid them where I could deal with them later. I took my shirt off as well. I opened the dryer, found a towel, and wiped my face. I found a pair of slacks and a T-shirt in the dryer and put those on.

I expected Tina to be awake, to ask where I was. But she was asleep, where I left her.

I went upstairs to use the bathroom. I looked at myself in the mirror. I looked horrible. I took my clean clothes off and had a quick shower, washing the smell of my neighbor from my hair. I brushed my teeth, to get her taste out. Naked, I went downstairs to the bedroom, and slipped into bed next to

Tina. She stirred, and nuzzled against me. I started kissing her. She kissed me back. She was half-awake as I mounted her, and went back to sleep after I quickly spilled my seed, grateful for that much needed fast relief.

The phone rang at ten-thirty in the morning. I had a bad hangover.

"Did you enjoy it?" her voice said. "Did you like last night? I *bet* you did. I know *I* did."

"Who is this?"

"Who the hell do you *think* this is?" Her accent was heavier. "No need to act *coy*, Mr. Lansdale. The wifey is at work, the son is at school, it's just you and the cute little girl with the dinosaur."

Jessica was, in fact, sitting on the living room floor and playing with her dinosaurs, making dinosaur roar sounds out of her mouth, making her dinosaurs fight, and then kiss and make up.

I took the cordless phone into the kitchen. I could hear Cassandra Payne breathing.

"What are you doing?" she said.

"Getting a glass of water." I turned on the faucet, and filled it with water. I drank.

"Feeling parched?"

"A little."

"I'm going to have to get the carpet dry-cleaned," she said, and laughed.

It was then that I knew last night wasn't an alcohol-induced hallucination. I rubbed my right temple.

"Come over," her voice said.

"What?"

"*What*," she mimicked me. "I said come over."

"My daughter is—"

"Bring her."

"No," I said. I couldn't believe she'd suggest such a thing. Then again—I could.

"It won't take long. Come over," she said, *"now."*

I peeked in on Jessica. She'd be okay for a few minutes, she always was. "All right," I said, and hung up the phone. I went outside.

Cassandra opened the door before I knocked. She grabbed me by the shirt and pulled me in. She was in a black bra and thong underwear. She kissed me on the mouth. It was a long kiss, our tongues attacking each other the way Jessica was making her dinosaurs attack each other: an age-old battle. The kiss went on for a good few minutes. I ran my hands up and down her body, feeling her taut, thin frame.

"I want to fuck you," I said.

"No," she said. "I just wanted a good morning kiss. Now get back home and watch your little girl."

I didn't want to go, of course. She pointed at the door and said, "Leave, now." I did as she mandated.

Walking across the street, I wondered if Bryan saw me. I had a weird feeling someone was watching what I was doing.

Jessica was still playing.

I don't think Bryan knew anything, and if he did, he was doing a good job of concealing it. Cassandra left in her car half an hour following our kissing encounter. Forty-five minutes later, Bryan came over and we began our ritual of drinking beers.

"Lawrence Payne's funeral is tomorrow morning," he said.

I nodded. He knew something, he just wasn't going to say it.

"The more I think about this, the more I don't like it," he said very carefully.

"What do you mean?"

"A murderer, living across the street from me. From you. From all of us. We're good, law-abiding people, Philip. We're good people. And she's a killer."

I didn't remind him that this was something we speculated, and not a fact.

"I used to be a cop," he said softly.

I knew he still wanted to be. I could understand—there were many things I wished I still was.

During dinner, I answered the phone. I looked at the Caller ID and recognized the number, because I'd seen it earlier today.

"Good, you answered," Cassandra Payne said.

Tina was talking to Matthew about something.

I turned away and lowered my voice. "Now isn't—"

"Hush. You don't need to talk. Just listen, you *per*vert. You like to peep? *Peep* on me tonight. At midnight. No, make it twelve-thirty, make sure wifey is in snoreland. Come to my window. We'll play and we'll have fun and we'll see what happens, hmm?"

She hung up.

"Who was it?" Tina asked.

"David," I said. "About the game Saturday."

"You're going to play?"

"The stomachache is gone," I said.

"But the gut isn't," she laughed. Jessica laughed with her. Matthew looked at me, wanting to know what was so funny.

I glanced down at my growing belly. It was looking bad. What did a woman like Cassandra Payne see in an aging, bloating guy like me?

Still, I was at her window at twelve-thirty sharp.

"I know you're out there, Mr. Lansdale," she said, "and don't say, 'I want to make love to you' or 'fuck you' or 'poke you' or whatever terminology you feel like employing tonight. Go back home now. Tomorrow, I bury my husband's remains.

I have to get a good night's sleep, I have to prepare for a very tedious and sad day. His family has come in from England, you know. They wanted his body flown over there, but Lawrence wanted to be buried here, if he died. That's what he always told me. 'Don't bury me back home,' he once said, 'bury me in America.' Which is what I'm going to do."

She came to the window, on her knees. I wanted to kiss her.

"Friday night, Mr. Lansdale," she said, "come back Friday night at the same time, and let's see how we shall transgress our little affair."

That word. Affair. I guess this was what it was—I was being unfaithful to my wife, in certain ways, in many ways. I was committing adultery and I wanted to keep doing it and I wanted to "transgress."

In the morning, I questioned myself. I told myself about all the trouble this could cause—to my life, my peace, to everything. And she was most likely a murderess; she didn't seem to be taking her husband's death too hard.

She was gone most of Thursday, picked up in the morning by a limousine, dressed all in black—plain black dress, shoes, hat, and veil, she was the mourning wife.

That afternoon, Bryan said, "Maybe it's time I dropped the hint to the boys in Homicide."

"Now?" I said. "So soon?" I pictured her in jail, far from my reach, and spending my life never knowing what it was like to be inside her.

"I'm having a real headache with this," he said. "A moral problem. *I used to be a cop.* I know, I say that a lot. I can't get this off my mind. I have to tell Homicide what we think, and let those boys take it from there."

"I think we should still wait," I said.

"She's burying the man today. Next, she'll gather up his assets, the insurance, and split back to England. Or maybe some other country without extradition. She'll get away with the perfect murder, and we can't let her do that."

"No, we can't."

"If the cops find her to be a suspect—*if* they let her know she's a suspect—"

"So she's not?" I said.

"Not?"

"A suspect. In their eyes."

He started to pace. "Not that I can determine. Why would they think so? They think she's the poor unfortunate widow."

"Maybe she is," I said. "Maybe we're wrong."

Bryan said, "We can't be wrong. She lied about not leaving that day. And there's the sneaky fellow from Las Vegas—"

I nodded.

"Still," he said.

"A few more days," I said, "that'd be good." I felt like I was convincing him.

He nodded, and cracked open a beer. "A few more days, and then we'll see what happens. I have a feeling in my gut something is going to transpire that will crack this mystery. It's an exciting feeling, huh, boy? Gives you goosebumps."

"Yeah."

Early that night, as my kids ate dinner, I noticed the black limo drop Cassandra Payne home.

Tina returned at one o'clock in the morning. I was sitting in my office. She was drunk. She hadn't driven home. She'd taken a taxi. But I didn't notice the taxi, or the time.

She stood at the door to my office. "I'm sorry," Tina said. "I didn't call. You must've been worried. You were waiting up for me."

"What?" I looked at the clock. "It's late."

"The girls and I got carried away. Little too much to drink, wasn't watching the time. I'm sorry."

"Are you okay?"

"I did the smart thing and took a taxi home."

"Where's your car?"

"At the bar. We'll have to get it in the morning."

"Okay."

"You're not mad at me?"

I smiled. "These things happen, honey."

"I'm ready to go to bed. Do you want to go to bed?"

We went to bed together. She smelled like alcohol, and so did I.

"I kinda feel like shit," Tina said.

So did I.

"It's the booze," she said. "We're drinking too much, Philip. Maybe we should stop."

My wife and I lived in different worlds.

She wanted to fool around. We kissed and touched.

"How come you never flirt with me?" she said.

"What's that?"

"You know, flirt."

"Married people don't flirt."

"I don't see why not," she said.

I couldn't do it. I wasn't in the mood for martial intercourse. Tina used her mouth, which always worked in the past, but not tonight.

"I'm sorry," I said.

She kissed me. "These things happen, honey. I'm tired anyway. Good night."

"Good night."

It was two o'clock.

She paid for her extravagance in the morning. Her head was pounding and spinning. She called into work sick, saying it'd be okay because her supervisor, a woman, was with her last night and would understand. I took Matthew to school, left Jessica with her mother. Coming back, I saw that Cassandra Payne's car was gone. Where'd she go so early? Tina was making coffee.

"Shouldn't you be in bed?" I asked.

She said, "I'm feeling better. I took some Advil."

She showered, and we drove to the bar she was at last night. Jessica played with her dinosaurs and Pokémon in the backseat. The bar was in Pacific Beach, two blocks from the ocean. It looked more like a club.

"I pictured you and the girls in some small, quiet hide-away," I said, "not a hip and happening joint like this."

"It's always somewhere different every week," she said softly.

That afternoon, she decided to go into work after all, call it half a day. She didn't like sitting around the house when she had a lot of cases piled up. She was afraid of getting behind, she said. I nodded. The only thing on my mind was twelve-thirty.

At twelve-thirty, I was at her window.

Before I left, I asked, "When will we meet next?"

She said, "I'll let you know."

"Good night," I said.

"Cheerio," Mrs. Payne said.

12

She showed up at the baseball game Saturday afternoon. It was the last thing I expected. But I wasn't surprised; she was a woman of unpredictable conduct.

I don't know how long she'd been sitting in the bleachers. David pointed her out to me, as we left the field and it was our team's turn at bat. "Isn't that our neighbor?" he said, and pointed. He seemed uncomfortable about her presence. It was her all right, in khaki slacks and a tank top, wearing those damn sunglasses, and a scarf around her head, like she was being incognito. She didn't acknowledge me when I looked right at her.

"What the hell is she doing here?" David said.

"I don't know," I said.

In the dugout, I told Bryan.

He turned, saw her, and said, "Oh shit." He made a face, and shook his head.

"It's her," I said.

Bryan was gradually becoming visibly upset. "It sure *is*. Now why the *hell* would *she* be *here*?"

"I don't know," I said, softly.

"She's never been here before, has she?" he asked.

"I don't believe so."

"How does she know about our games?"

I didn't know that either. I certainly didn't tell her.

"This is odd," Bryan said.

"Yeah."

"Something's fishy," he said. "Something smells like halibut."

I felt self-conscious knowing she was watching, and terrified not knowing why she was here. I was scared that she was up to something, that she had a plan, that maybe she was now plotting *my* murder. It occurred to me, then, that she was doing her own spying, when I thought I was being pretty clever.

I sucked in my gut when I went up to bat. I wanted to impress her, and there was no one else here to impress—neither my wife nor my kids were all that interested in Saturday's middle-aged men's ball game. I wanted to hit a home run just for her—I wanted to hear her cheer and, hell, I wanted to hear the whole small crowd roar. I wanted to knock that ball right out of the park.

I was trying too hard. I struck out.

The Fritzes lost the game.

I didn't want to face her in this defeat. I imagined she'd smile, kiss my nose, and say, "It's only a game, Mr. Lansdale."

But she was gone.

After a game—victory or defeat—the team always went to this certain sports pub and grill that had cheap beer and great food. I just wanted a few pints and a bacon cheeseburger . . . and sink into a corner.

Bryan wouldn't leave me alone.

He sat with me, and his expression was grave. I wondered where David was, he seemed to have just disappeared.

"Philip," he said, "this is bad."

"How we lost?" I was being facetious; I knew what he was referring to.

"*That* was bad," he said, grinning for a moment. He leaned forward, drinking his beer. The grin was gone. "I mean Mrs. Payne. She must be on to us."

"How could she?" I said. "Does she have bugs in our homes? Does she know every move we make, every conversation we have?"

"She's observant and smart," he said. "Every killer is extremely cautious after the crime. There's no other explanation. Her being there today was no coincidence."

I couldn't argue. "No. It wasn't."

"She was giving us a message," he said.

"A message? And what is the message?"

"She was saying, 'I know you've been watching me, so now I'm watching you.' It was like a warning."

"Come on, Bryan," I laughed, "you're getting carried away." I didn't want to tell him that these were my exact thoughts. I could have told him the truth right then and there, and maybe that would've cleared up the mystery. I didn't have the courage to tell him. I felt small, sitting across from this ex-cop who had more balls than I ever would.

I realized that there were many traits in Bryan that I admired, and that I would like to have in my own makeup—but it'd never be. I was a coward, a louse, and I was putting our investigation into jeopardy.

I never would have made it as a cop. I couldn't make it as a lawyer.

"Then *you* tell me why she was at the game, Mr. Smarts," Bryan said, snapping me out of my self-pity. "You give me a good reason."

I wanted to. I wanted to say, *Maybe because I'm fooling around with her.*

"I'm going to have to tell Roger," Bryan said.

"You think you should?" My spine was crawling.

"For our sake, yes."

"She's not some psycho killer," I said.

"How do we *know* this?"

I drank my beer.

Bryan said, "He's out of town. Roger. Family thing. Monday, I'll tell him what we suspect, what we know, and he can take it from there."

That night, after midnight, the phone rang once.

I was lying in bed.

Ten minutes later, it rang once again.

Tina was sound asleep. I went into the kitchen, to the caller

ID machine. It was *her* number. Before I could call her, it rang again, and I quickly picked it up.

"You're there," she said softly.

"You shouldn't call at this hour."

She giggled. "Did I wake the kids?"

"You—"

"You looked cute in the baseball uniform today," she said.

"So you were there."

"You *know* I was."

"You didn't stick around."

"A bit awkward if I did. And you were losing."

"Yeah."

"*Badly.*"

"Don't rub it in," I said. "What were you doing there?"

"It's a public place," she said. "Do I not have a right, as a member of the public?"

"You know what I mean."

"Did you think I followed you? How vain. Maybe I was there for a completely different reason."

"What reason?"

She giggled some more. "I followed you there. I saw you leave your house in that cute uniform and I decided to follow you. It seems fair—you've been watching me, now I am watching you."

Bryan was closer to the truth than he understood.

"Then again," she said, "maybe I was there to watch some-one else."

I said, "I wanted to hit a home run for you."

"Isn't that sweet." She blew a kiss over the phone.

I said, "I want to come over."

"Twenty minutes ago," she said, "I was in the mood. The moment has passed. I'm going to bed. You'll have to wait."

"Wait? When?"

"Monday night. Same time."

"Why not tomorrow night?" I asked.

"I'm busy all day tomorrow. I doubt," she said, "I shall feel amorous."

"What are you doing tomorrow?"

"That's *my* business, and *my* business alone."

"And what if I just came over right now? If I just marched over there and took you in my arms?"

"Don't," she said and she hung up.

Maybe she was playing a game; maybe she wanted to see if I was aggressive and would take control of the situation. I thought better of it. She was a woman who enjoyed control. And I didn't want to risk experiencing her rejection.

13

She wasn't home all Sunday. She left early, came home late. I imagined she was with another man—perhaps this Boyd Urick character from Las Vegas. I was jealous and knew it was an absurd thing to feel. If anything, I should've been ashamed of myself—

And I was. It may not seem like it, but I was. I was good at bottling it in. I knew that what I was doing was wrong, foolish, dangerous, and just plain stupid. I knew my actions would hurt Tina, would hurt my kids, would injure my entire family. I knew that something wasn't right with Cassandra Payne that she could launch into such a sexual tryst right after her husband's murder. Still, I coveted her; still, I didn't want our encounters to stop. I was thinking with my prick, which is the worst thing any man in history can allow to think for him—it leads to an ugly road, and in my case, an ugly road in the middle of the night deep in the desert.

I counted every minute until the appointed hour that Monday night. I had a fresh bottle of Wild Turkey that I was going to bring, to share; and I knew that I would—finally— fuck her.

I looked into the window.

She was playing the music, she had on the robe, she had an empty glass in hand, she was dancing about the bedroom.

"What light on yonder window breaks," I whispered into the screen.

"Romeo? Romeo?" she said. "Is it truly you, Mr. Romeo?"

"It is I," said I, "bearing gifts."

She told me to come inside, the door was unlocked. I did.

Again, the candle. I held out the bottle. She got a glass for me, from the kitchen, and we poured bourbon and drank. We kissed. I caressed her breasts, I rubbed my hand between her legs, but she kept eluding any attempts I made to entice her into the bedroom, on the couch, on the goddamn floor! "Silly goose," she said, holding her glass out for more to drink.

She turned the volume up on the soft jazz, told me she wanted to dance. "I'll watch you dance any time," I said, but she told me she wanted me to dance with her. I wasn't a good dancer, I informed her of this, but I was too drunk to care, and she certainly didn't care. *We danced.* Our bodies close to one another, we moved to the music, to the night, and to the alcohol in our bloodstream. She took my shirt off and sucked on my nipples, gently biting them and causing me to jump. She laughed. I bit her nipples in turn, and she liked this.

We didn't fuck. There was kissing, there was touching, there was mutual oral sex, but still she would not allow me to fuck her. When I asked her why, she said it wasn't time, and when it *was* time, she would let me know. I was past the point of caring, naked with her, dancing still, most of the bottle of Wild Turkey gone, and my brain was again spinning with lust and booze.

Then it was time to go. "Jesus Christ," I said, when I noticed it was four in the morning.

"Time does fly, yes?" she said.

I kissed her good-bye, and said, "Until next time, Juliet."

"Next time, Romeo," she said, but didn't say when that would be.

Tina was awake when I got into bed. "Where were you?"

I didn't know what to say. Had she heard me come in through the back? I'd been very careful; maybe I was clumsy. I'd taken it for granted that she'd be deep asleep as she always was.

"Philip?"

"Yeah?"

"Where were you?"

"What do you mean, where was I?" I was so nervous, I should've given up right then and there.

She said, "I woke up and you weren't here and I looked all over the house and you were nowhere. Your car was outside. I was worried."

"Did you think the boogeyman took me?" Always make jokes when you get caught.

"Where *were* you?" she said. She was very serious.

"I was in my office," I lied.

"I looked in your office. It was dark and empty."

"I was also in the backyard."

"I knew you were outside. I heard you coming in."

"I was looking for meteors," I said.

"What?"

"I heard on the news there'd be a meteor shower between two and four." I thought it sounded convincing; I liked star-gazing and she knew it.

"Bullshit," she said. She moved near me, and sniffed. "You've been drinking. I can smell it on you."

Could she smell Cassandra Payne on me? I could. I should've taken a shower.

"Yeah," I said.

"Were you outside drinking with Bryan and watching for meteors?"

"Bryan is asleep."

"Did you see a meteor?"

"No," I said, waiting for a fight.

She sighed. "You've been drinking too much lately."

"Yeah."

"So have I," she said. "Philip, I think we're turning into alcoholics."

"Not us."

"I think so."

"We're okay."

"It's strange that I couldn't find you. I even looked out back."

"Did you go out back?"

"No."

"I was there."

"I didn't see you."

"It's dark." I was being the lawyer again, twisting the scenario in my favor.

"I don't like this," she said.

"Go to sleep, now," I said, gently.

I didn't expect her to stop asking me questions, but she said, "Okay," and went back to sleep.

I had a hard time sleeping. I wondered if Tina believed me or not, and if it mattered. I had taken a shower before going back to bed, to get any telltale smells off my body—perfume and sex.

If Tina suspected anything, she didn't let on; she acted as if our life was normal and usual. I kissed her good-bye and and sent her off to work and then I took my son to school and came back home and played dinosaurs with my daughter.

I waited all day for Cassandra Payne to call, to give me a signal, about when we would meet next—tonight perhaps, although I realized that would be outrageous, to do such a thing the night after my wife almost caught me.

There was something also exciting about it . . .

The widow Mrs. Payne didn't leave all day. Bryan and I drank beers and watched the house out of the corner of our eyes. We were being too obvious, I thought. This is how she knows.

Bryan was antsy—standing, sitting, looking nervous. He kept cracking his knuckles.

Where was David? He'd been scarce lately. I asked Bryan about him.

"I'm not his fucking keeper," he snapped at me, "how should I know?"

"Relax," I told him.

"I told Roger," he said.

This I didn't want to hear. "What did he say?"

"Not much."

"What was the expression on his face?"

"Goddamn lawyer," he smiled, and sat down. "I don't know. I told him over the phone."

"He didn't say anything?"

"He said something to the effect that I had an interesting theory and he would look into it."

I felt relieved. "He doesn't buy it."

"He thinks I'm full of shit."

"*We* could be full of shit," I said.

He frowned, looking away. "We could."

I want us to be.

Past midnight, I watched her house and drank vodka. There was no signal. There was no light on, no soft music seeping out and reaching my ears.

I slept next to my wife.

Wednesday yielded no contact from her as well. I almost called her—I had her number. Instinctively, I knew she would be angry if I phoned. I decided that if I didn't hear from her today, I would call her tomorrow.

Early in the evening, an Oldsmobile pulled up in front of her house. A man in a cheap suit, with a strong build, got out. I recognized him as one of the Homicide cops that had been there before: Bryan's connection in the department, Roger. I didn't know if Roger was his last or first name. I was frightened, aghast. I was afraid for her—what would happen to her? Would they give her life, the death sentence, if she was guilty? I wanted to run across the street and tell the cop that everything Bryan said to him was a ruse. This was why he was here, wasn't he? Following up on Bryan's information, to check if she'd been lying about not leaving her house the night in question, to see if there was some motive for wanting her husband dead.

Tina knew something was wrong. It must've been pulsating off my body. At dinner, she said, "What is it?"

"What is what?" I said.

"Something heavy is on your mind."

I couldn't deny it. "Things have changed."

"I know."

"I mean, they need to," I said. "I should go back to work."

She looked at her food and said, "Maybe that's a good idea."

The unmarked police car didn't leave all night. What the hell was going on in there? With another bottle of vodka, I sat in my office and watched the house. The lights were on, occasionally I saw a body—his, hers—walk about. What were they talking about? This was torture. At eleven-fifty, the living room light went off. At last, he was going to leave. He didn't. The bedroom light to the side was on. I drank. It was twelve-twenty. I couldn't take it anymore. I had to know what was going on. I snuck out back and went across the street. Going there, I knew what I would see, I *knew* what had transpired, I knew why this detective had been there for hours, so I shouldn't have been surprised when I looked into the window and saw the two of them naked. I was angry—and it wasn't just for the reason that she'd lured this man into bed (and who could blame him, with the prospect of a beautiful woman?), but that he was fucking her; he was on top of her, her legs were on his muscular, defined shoulders, and he was slamming his pelvis hard into hers, so hard I could hear their flesh slapping together, and she was crying out, "Oh yes, baby, yes," and he was grunting and all I wanted to know was why did the bitch let this man behold the pleasure she'd deprived me of?

The detective left early in the morning. I started drinking after my few hours of restless, Cassandra-filled sleep. In my dreams, she was letting every man I'd ever known fuck her, and she made me watch while I was tied to a chair.

I was testy with Jessica, telling her to leave me alone, telling her to shut up as I paced around the house. She looked at me with her sad, large eyes and I felt just horrible. There was no reason for my child to suffer any recriminations for my own lack of fidelity. Still, I obsessed over the woman across the street, allowing my desires—my cock—to guide me. I had no interest in sitting around with either Bryan or David today. Bryan said, "We need to talk," and I said, "We'll talk tomorrow," and he said, "I think we should talk today," and I said, "We'll talk tomorrow." I was a menace to society, driving around, almost causing two accidents, picking up Matthew from school. He seemed to know that there was something wrong—he kept glaring at me and wouldn't say a word. He glared at me at the dinner table. Dinner was also a mess, hastily slopped together macaroni and cheese. Tina wasn't there, it was Thursday, bar night for the girls. Jessica played with her dinosaurs. A sitcom was on TV. I wanted to scream. I wanted to run. When the kids settled into sleep, I was thankful. I sat outside with a bottle of something and watched, waiting for my signal. Nothing came, and I was too drunk to do anything even if she called me over, having binged all day, feeling like I was going to vomit. I went to bed; I don't know what time it was, I simply fell on the mattress and closed my eyes and when I woke up—the bedroom light came on—Tina was standing there, staring down at me. She was a bit drunk herself, and disheveled—hair messy, lipstick smeared, blouse torn. Focusing my eyes, I noticed scratches on her face and chest, a small cut on her lower lip. It was past four in the morning.

"Didn't even wait up for me this time?" she said. "Didn't wonder and worry where I was?"

"Tina?"

"That's me." She made a silly pose, and giggled.

"What happened to you?"

She turned and looked in the mirror. "Oh God." She touched her face. "Oh God, I got carried away." She giggled again, then started to cry. It was very abrupt.

I sat up. "Tina—"

She turned, pointing. "Don't come near me, you! You! *Don't* you *even* come near me!"

I stood, swaying, feeling sick again.

She said, "You wanna know where I was? You wanna know what I was doing? I'll tell you. *I was getting laid!*"

I could feel it coming up from my stomach, the goddamn macaroni and cheese.

"That's right!" my wife said. "I got screwed! I got fucked! And by a younger man! He was twenty-five, I think, a construction worker, all tan and muscle and delicious! He flirted with me at the bar! Yes he did! Other men have too! But this was the first time I left with anyone. This is the first time I've ever done anything like this! I went to his apartment with him—"

"He raped you?"

"He didn't *rape* me, you idiot! You stupid *ass*hole! *I* attacked *him!* Oh yeah I guess I look like I've been through a storm but I'll tell you that it was rough sex and it was great! We broke his lamp! I think we broke his *bed!* I *like* it rough, Philip! I bet you never knew that about me! Before we met, I liked it rough! *Real rough!* Rougher than this! I thought rough sex had no place in a marriage but I was wrong!" She picked up a shoe and threw it at me. It missed. "Tell me," she said, "does that Limey bitch like it rough?"

I saw my reflection in the mirror. I was ghost pale white.

"Don't stand there all shocked and 'who me?' you jack-asshole," she went on. "You don't think I know? You think I didn't know all this time? I knew from the start! I knew the day of our little barbecue, when she walked in, the way you looked at her, the way you swooned, the way you fucked her with your eyes! *Optical intercourse!*" she yelled. "Eyeball fuckorama!" She threw her other shoe at me. I dodged that one, barely. I knew I was going to throw up any minute now. "I knew you were across the street the other night! I knew you were with that Limey bitch! That—that—*London whore!* How long has it been going on, Philip? *How long?* Tell me! Before or after her husband died?"

I felt like I was going to faint.

"What she sees in you, I don't know. Lazy, beer-gut booze hound you do nothing all day but mope around about your sorry sad lost career! A good career you fucked up! A disgraced lawyer! A disbarred shyster! A cheating husband! So my husband is fucking my neighbor, well I'll show him! I'll go out and fuck someone too! And that's what I did, Philip! And you know what, I don't even know the kid's name! And you know what? The whole time I was doing it, when he was fucking me and I was fucking him, the whole time, and after, and when I was driving home, I told myself, 'I'm going to tell him what I did and let's see how that makes him feel!' And I'm telling. I'm telling you, Philip. Not half an hour ago I was fucking and sucking and licking and rolling and poking and squirting and everything else you can imagine with another man."

"I never fucked her," I blurted, and ran to the bathroom, and puked in the sink.

———

I slept on the couch. It was easy to sleep, pretend that none of this ever happened. I felt like I wasn't in my body. I was watching myself move about, pouring a bowl of cereal for Matthew, making coffee for Tina and myself. She'd covered the scratches on her face with makeup, and there was a scab on her lip now. We didn't say anything to each other for a while. It didn't take too long for her to break the silence.

"You have nothing to say?"

"No," I replied.

Then she went at it again, yelling and screaming, throwing her coffee cup against the wall, cracking it in two, brown fluid seeping down the flower-print wallpaper. What Tina said was pretty much the same thing—in different order and more cussing—that she had said at four in the morning. My head was pounding. I couldn't take it anymore. I grabbed her by the arms and pleaded for her to shut up. I shook her like a rag doll, her head bobbing back and forth. She started kicking at and me and calling me names.

A shrill scream stopped us. It was Matthew, sitting at the table. The high-pitched sound that came out of his gaping mouth went on for a minute. Tina and I just stared at him, my hands still wrapped around her arms, her hair all over her face. Then Matthew yelled, *"Stop it! Stop it! Stop it!"* and threw his glass of milk at us. Tina and I were covered in milk. Jessica started crying.

"Now look what you did," Tina said.

"Me?"

"*You*," she said, freeing herself from my grip. "I'm going."

Matthew was still screaming and Jessica was crying.

I followed Tina to the living room. "You're going? Looking like that you're going?"

"I'm not going to work. I can't possibly go to work. I don't know where I'm going but I'm going."

"Back to the construction worker's apartment? Back to screw him?"

She glared at me. "Maybe I am."

"What about the kids? You're leaving them, the way they are?"

"You explain it to them," she said as she went out the door, "it's your fault all this happened."

She burned rubber as she left.

Matthew and Jessica settled down. Matthew looked at me, expressionless, arms folded, while Jessica gave me a quizzical glance with her large wet eyes.

I started to clean up the milk on the floor. The glass hadn't broken and I found myself grateful for that. "Everything's okay now," I said, and it was probably the biggest lie I'd ever uttered, and I wasn't even a lawyer anymore.

Matthew kept his arms folded as I drove him to school. He slammed the car door shut as he left. I drove slowly back home, trying to piece the last twenty-four hours together. I thought I'd be sick again.

"Don't fight anymore, Daddy," Jessica said.

"That's good advice," I said.

Cassandra Payne's car was gone. I'd had every intention to have it out with her, to have some final and parting words, to tell her what she'd done to my life, and now I was going to have to wait. Bryan came over, knocked on the door, but I didn't answer. He phoned—it was his number on the Caller ID—but I didn't pick up. His voice on the answering machine said: "Philip, what's going on? We need to talk."

I picked Matthew up from school later in the afternoon. Neither Cassandra nor my wife had returned yet. Matthew still wouldn't talk, he only glared, like I was the lowest piece of shit that ever existed in San Diego. Maybe I was. I was expecting Bryan to confront me, either as I left or returned, but he didn't. There was no sign of him.

An hour later, and a few beers in me, Cassandra drove up in her car.

She was wearing a black mini and a cut-off top, high heels, looking like a hooker. I rushed across the street before she went inside.

"Mr. Lansdale!" she said, acting surprised.

"Don't play coy," I had her by the arm, "let's go inside, right now."

"Rather pushy," she said.

"You bet I am."

She didn't fight me. She got out her keys and we went inside.

"Would you like a drink?" she asked.

"No," I said.

"You look like you need a drink."

"That's the last thing I need."

"I know I need a drink." She went to the bar in the living room. It was well stocked. I didn't know she had a bar. I'd never seen the place in daylight. The furniture was clean and looked new, looked unlived in. Everything about the house was spotless. Did she keep it up like this herself? I'd never seen any maids come and go. She poured herself two shots of Wild Turkey. I asked for some. She handed me a glass.

I said to her, "Do you know what you've done to my life?"

"I've done nothing to your life. You do what you do of your own free will, and none of it has a damn thing to do with me, love."

She sounded like she knew. Maybe she heard Tina and me fighting. Maybe she *did* have bugs planted in my home.

"Forget that," I said, and added, "you slut."

"Slut, is it now?"

"Fucking the cops now?"

She smiled. "Naughty person. Peeping Philip."

"That's right," I said. "That cop was here pretty long the other night. I saw . . ."

"You came and took a gander into my yonder window break?" she laughed.

"Yes . . ."

"And what did your dirty little peepers see?"

"I saw you fucking him."

"He was a good hard fuck," she said. "A strong, handsome man with a strong manly man smell. How could a silly little horny girl like me resist such a temptation?"

"Why? *Why?*"

"Why?" she said, frowning.

"Why did you give it to him," I said, "and not me? After all the times I begged you for it?"

She seemed very amused. "You mean my cunt?"

"*Yes!*"

And with that, she threw her head back and laughed. I watched the muscles of her neck ripple.

"You're quite silly, you know," she said.

"Goddamn you," I said, feeling myself near a breakdown, "goddamn you—"

"And what if I *am* a slut? You have nothing on me, Mr. Lansdale, you're a married cheating man and I'm a grieving widow. I'll sleep with whom I please, thank you."

"Why him, and not me?"

She poured herself another shot. "If you see something you want, why don't you be a man and just take it?"

I did. I threw my glass aside, bourbon staining her carpet, and rushed her. I grabbed her arms. I didn't shake her like I'd done to Tina this morning. I kissed her. I kissed her hard. I bit her lip, drawing blood, and she liked this, and I realized this is what must've happened between Tina and the man she was with last night. I threw Cassandra Payne to the floor— yes, threw, or pushed hard, I wasn't gentle, I was going to take what I wanted once and for all, and be done with her. She laughed as she went down. I lifted her mini and tore away her matching black panties.

I couldn't do it.

I'd finally reached my Nirvana, my Timbuktu, my salvation, and I began to weep. I don't know why I was crying—it all came out in a rush. Maybe because I knew this wasn't what I really, truly wanted. I didn't know *what* the hell I wanted, and that was what scared me. I was uncertain of the life I was leading, but I didn't want to lose that life. Being here with Cassandra, I was putting that life at risk. Tina had cheated on me, she'd been with another man, and it seemed right that I finally do the same and just fuck "the Limey bitch."

But I couldn't do it.

I cried like a baby, knowing it was all over now. She hushed and cooed me and kissed my ears.

"Let's run away," I said. It just came out of my mouth.

"Don't be a goose."

"Let's just run away," I mumbled, "and be together forever. I love you."

"You don't love me," she said, "you don't know what you're saying."

She knew the truth better than I, but still I was telling her how we should split from San Diego. I wanted out of my life. I wanted a *new* life.

She said, "Mr. Lansdale, you know nothing about me. Nothing at all."

"I know enough."

"You can't even see the tip of the iceberg," she said, "all you see is the illusion."

"I see you, and what I see is what I want."

"You don't know me," she said softly.

"I think I do," I said.

She laughed, and then sniffed. "Do you smell something burning?"

I did.

And I heard sirens in the distance.

"What is that smell?" she said.

"Oh Jesus God," I said.

I quickly pulled up my pants. I almost fell to the floor. Cassandra, half-naked, chased after me, wanting to know what was wrong. I knew, before I opened the door and went outside *I knew*. My house was on fire. Somewhere from the back, it was going up in smoke. The sirens were closer. Bryan stood on the sidewalk, looking at my house. Jessica was next to him. Matthew wasn't. Jessica turned and saw me. She yelled, *"Daddy!"* She started running toward me. Bryan reached to grab her, saying, "No!" He wasn't quick enough. Everything started to move very, very slowly at that moment. It was like a scene out of a de Palma film. The fire truck was coming around the corner, fast. Bryan was mouthing the word "no." Jessica was running toward me, arms out in fear, crying, wanting my protection. Cassandra Payne stood at her door, not bothering to cover herself, trying to piece the situation together. I looked at Jessica, then my house, then Bryan, then Cassandra, then Jessica, and then the fire truck. I started running for Jessica. She was in the middle of the street. The fire truck slammed on its brakes, the driver leaned on the booming horn, but it was too late. The truck hit her, and her little body flew into the air.

14

There was nothing the paramedics could do. Jessica was dead. The firemen found Matthew in the back, staring, mesmerized, at the destruction he'd started. He had a book of matches in his hand. He'd started burning some newspapers on the patio, and the old wood of the patio ignited, and the fire spread to the house. The patio was destroyed, as well as part of the kitchen. Tina came home as the fire was being extinguished and Jessica's body loaded in the ambulance. My wife started screaming. She was confused, she didn't understand. I knew how she felt. I noticed Cassandra watching from her window—a pale face, two eyes, dark hair. Then Bryan was restraining me—no, he and a fireman, holding my arms, holding me back. I don't know what I was screaming, who I wanted to attack. Tina was all over me, hitting me, spitting on me, and a police officer pulled her away. It was true, hellish pandemonium. Tina was crying, she was wailing, "My baby is dead! My little girl is dead!" and I saw Cassandra Payne's eyes again, across the street, another witness to the atrocity exhibition, and it dawned on me that, finally, yes, this was all my fault, I wasn't in the house watching over my children—my responsibility and duty; no I was in an act of sin, and for my sins, I had lost my child, and probably my wife, and most certainly my life as I knew it.

Jessica was officially pronounced dead at the hospital. Dazed, I signed various pieces of paperwork. Tina had to be sedated. I wanted to be sedated. I wanted to be put to sleep. My son was questioned by some sort of police psychologist. Bryan and Ellen were there. Tina's sister, Janet, showed up, and took the drugged Tina and stoic Matthew home with her.

"You can stay with us," Ellen told me.

"No," I said. "That's okay. I can go home."

"You sure, son?" Bryan said.

"It's my home," I said.

They drove me back. They still tried to convince me to sleep in one of their guest rooms. I thanked them. I said I needed to be home, and I needed to be alone.

I wanted the darkness and quiet of my shattered house. I wanted the anguish, because I deserved it. So this was the price. I noticed that Cassandra's car was gone. What was she feeling? Did she experience any guilt over this? Why the fuck was I even thinking of her?

I wanted to cry but I couldn't. It was like I had no eyes.

I wanted to scream but I couldn't. It was like I had no mouth.

I sat in the darkness, in the living room. On the floor were Jessica's plastic dinosaurs; they were waiting for her to return home and play with them.

I wasn't aware of time.

The sun rose, the birds sang.

People drove off to work.

The phone rang several times. I didn't move. I was numb. I was so damn numb.

When I did move, I turned on the TV. Cartoons. I stared at the TV. Jessica liked cartoons, all children do. Would she really never watch cartoons again?

I told myself I had to eat. I went into the kitchen, which was was pretty much burnt wood, but the fridge and phone and Caller ID machine were still there.

The phone rang.

"Yes?"

"Philip," Bryan said, "we'll talk now."

"Okay."

I went out the front, to meet him. I didn't want him in the

house, I didn't want him to see the cause and effect of my
fuck-ups.

I decided I would tell him the truth about what I had done.

He walked over, as a black 1971 Ford Mustang pulled into
the Paynes' driveway. Cassandra's Taurus still wasn't there. I
had no idea if she'd come home and left or not. A bald black
man with shades and a trench stepped out of the car. He was
big. His bald head was shiny. Bryan and I both watched him
as he went to the Paynes' door and kicked it in. He didn't
knock, he *kicked*, and went inside.

"What the hell," Bryan said.

A minute later the man came out. Bryan walked across the
street to confront him.

"No," I whispered.

"You!" Bryan yelled. *"You!"*

"Bryan," I said, "don't—"

The man stopped, cocked his head, and regarded Bryan.

"Yes you," Bryan said. "Just what in all *hell* do you think
you're doing, mister?"

"Collecting," the man said.

"You can't just bust into people's houses in broad daylight
like that!" Bryan was face to face with the man—well, Bryan's
head reached the man's chest.

"I can't?" said the man. "Should I have waited until night-
fall?" He laughed.

"What's the meaning of this? What are you doing here?"

"Doesn't concern you, pops." The man was trying to get to
his car and Bryan was blocking his path.

"Oh yes it does," Bryan was saying. "This is *my* neighborhood and I'm not about to allow this sort of thing to happen!"

"Whatcha gonna do about it, pops?"

"Who are you, and *what* are you doing here?"

"You sure are full of questions," said the man.

"Who are you?" Bryan said again, his voice shaking.

"Who are you?" the man asked flatly.

"I used to be a police officer," Bryan said with pride.

"I'm *so* impressed, pops."

"Since I'm a citizen now, I am hereby making a citizen's arrest."

"Citizen's arrest this, pops." The man reached into his trench coat, pulled out a gun as black as the trench and the Mustang, and fired. There was a silencer on the gun, it went puff puff puff—the first bullet into Bryan's knee. Bryan fell back on his ass. The second bullet was in Bryan's shoulder, the third in his chest. The man looked over at me. I thought he was going to shoot me, too. He got into his Mustang and calmly drove away.

Bryan was squirming and bleeding on the Paynes' driveway.

I was unruffled, and surprised how well I took this new sequence of events. Still quite numb, I turned around, walked into my house, and called 911.

15

I was in the hospital again, same waiting room, same emergency wing, same goddamn hospital. Next, I knew, it would be me in here.

I was with Ellen, holding her hand. Or maybe she was holding my hand. I was numb, she was shaking. "He'll pull through, he'll pull through," she kept saying, nodding her head; maybe she was praying. She didn't ask me any questions, like why was a man with a gun at the Paynes', breaking and entering and shooting her husband?

It'd certainly been a busy week on my block. "The Cursed Neighborhood" one TV newscaster called it. Aside from the sensationalist value, there was truth to this.

In the wee hours of the morning, a doctor came out and told us that Bryan was alive, but in critical condition.

"Will he pull through?" Ellen asked.

"It's hard to say. We have to wait and see," said the doctor. "He's a fighter, your husband."

"Yes he is." She smiled.

"He's conscious. He's been asking for you both."

He didn't look too good, in the ICU, tubes and wires coming out of his arms, nose, and mouth. Ellen wept, and carefully embraced him. He told her he would pull through and she told him *you better*, as if there would be some sort of punishment if he'd died.

"Honey," he said, straining each word, "I—need—to—talk—to—Philip—private. Please—give—us—five—minutes."

"No," she said.

"Please."

"Why?"

"We—have—to discuss—the case," he said.

"Damn you, Bryan," she said. "Couldn't you leave things alone?" She looked at me. "The both of you?"

"Ellen," he said, weakly.

She nodded, and left us alone, wiping her eyes.

He looked at me. "She knows—what we've—been up to. Can't—keep any—secrets from her."

"Oh Christ, Bryan," I said, "this is all my fault."

"Don't—go—putting—world's—burden—on—your—shoulders—" and he coughed: "kid."

"I have to be honest with you." I pulled up a chair alongside him. "I was having . . . intimate contact with Cassandra Payne."

"I know," he said.

"You did?" I wasn't surprised.

"You—think—you—had—some—big secret?"

"Shit."

"That's," he coughed. "That's what—I wanted—to—talk to—you—about. Last—few days."

"*Shit.*"

"Was—gone—tell—you. Fucking—up. Fuck. Up."

"You got that—"

"Listen. Dangerous woman."

"I know."

"You—not the only one—she—she fools—with."

"What?"

"Stay away—from her."

"I will. But I think she's gone."

"Philip," he said.

"Yeah?"

"I'm—I'm not going—to—make it."

"*Don't* say that. You'll make it." It almost felt like I was going to get beyond that numb feeling, have an outburst, but it quickly retreated inside me.

"No," he coughed.

I said softly, "You'll make it."

"You—must. You—do something for me."

"Anything," I said. "Anything."

"Find my daughter," he said, strength returning to his voice. "Find Rachel. Listen. I want—find her—tell her." He breathed hard, trying to gain his voice. "Ellen will never look for her. Afraid—Ellen—afraid to. Of rejection. Find Rachel—tell her I forgive her. I—love her. Her mother—loves her. I die—Ellen will have—no one. She—will—need—Rachel. Tell—Rachel— what happened to me—and—I—never—stopped loving— her."

Then it came out. I was crying now, thinking of my own dead daughter. I was looking at Bryan like a father—and I guess he was. We were men who had much in common now. He let me cry, and I turned away.

"How will I find her?" I asked, after I had composed myself.

"Few years ago—I did—some looking," he said. "Last—I know—she was in—Chicago."

"Is she married?"

"Don't know. Will—you—find her—when I'm—"

"*If.*" He was getting me angry with this talk.

"Not going—to—make it—kid." His expression was sincere.

I was defeated. "I'll find her, I promise."

Bryan died several days later in the hospital from an internal hemorrhage. I wouldn't know about this until later, because at the time I was in Las Vegas close to my own death.

I went home after my talk with Bryan. I left Ellen with him. It was still dark out, and the sun was starting to rise as I drove.

Tina was home, packing things into two suitcases.

"Where are you going?" I asked.

"I didn't think you'd be home," she said. "Were you across the street balling the Limey bitch?"

"I was at the hospital. Bryan was shot."

She stopped what she was doing. "I saw it on the news. What the hell is happening here? What have you done, Philip? *What the hell have you done?* Bryan's a good man, a very good man—and you got him into something very bad."

She was right, of course.

"We think Mrs. Payne murdered her husband," I said. "We think a certain man was involved, but not the man who shot Bryan."

"*We?*"

"I don't know what's going on but it is bad," I said.

"But you were *fucking* her?" Tina said. "What was *that?* Part of your amateur detective work? Undercover? Playing James Fucking *Bond?*"

"I can't explain myself," I said. "I didn't—" I wanted to tell her the truth, but what did it matter?

"Our daughter is dead," my wife went on, "our son is a pyromaniac, your friend is in the hospital, and I'm going to divorce you." She started packing again.

"Don't do this," I said, moving toward her.

"*Don't you fucking come near me!*"

I backed away, hands up, scared and sad.

"Where's Matthew?" I asked after a moment.

"At Janet's. He's going to need psychiatric care, you realize this?"

Numb again, I said, "Yes."

She said, packing, "We're failures as parents. This *marriage* is a failure. I want to get out of San Diego. I want to divorce your ass, take my son, move far far away, and never see you ever again."

"You don't mean that."

"I never meant anything more in my life."

"Marry the construction worker," I said, and wished I hadn't.

"Jessica is dead!" she screamed. She turned and punched the wall. I knew it must've hurt.

We stood there, staring at one another.

"I'm sorry," I said.

"The fuck you are," she said, grabbing her two suitcases. She lugged them out to her car and drove away.

I was alone again.

I sat in front of the TV and watched it for hours. I had no idea what I was watching.

The phone rang. I stood, walked into the burnt kitchen, and picked it up. "Tina?"

"It's me," Cassandra Payne's voice said.

"So it is," I said. I knew she'd call, sooner or later.

"I heard about what happened to Mr. Vaughn."

"Yeah, and it happened on your property."

"I know." Her voice was very distant.

"Some man broke into your house."

"He was there to kill me," she said. "Most likely."

"Oh yeah? And why would he want to kill you?"

"It's a long and complex story."

"I like long and complex stories."

"I called to say . . . I'm very sorry." She sounded sincere.

"How sweet of you."

"I should hang up," she said.

"Why did you really call," I asked, adding, "you coldhearted bitch?"

"I'm not as coldhearted as you think," she said. "Maybe I am. But I am sorry. I never meant for anyone to get hurt. I didn't want this. I'm so sorry about your sweet little girl. It's my dream to have children but I never can. And I'm so sorry about Mr. Vaughn. He's injured because of me."

"It's because of me," I said.

"Good-bye, Mr. Lansdale."

"Wait. You're not coming back?"

"No. I imagine the police want to talk to me, yes?"

"Did you kill your husband?"

"You asked me that before," she said.

"You told me no."

"The answer is still no."

"So who was the bald man in the trench coat? Did *he* kill your husband?"

"I have to go now. We'll never see each other again, which is for the best. We should never have seen each other in the first place."

"Yeah? Why?"

"You know why, I believe you *know*," she said. "You don't want to admit it."

"Stop being so cryptic."

"Bloody Philip," she said, and hung up.

I looked at the Caller ID. The area code was 727. Nevada. I called the number.

"Stardust Hotel," a man said.

"Can I have Cassandra Payne's room, please?"

"Just a moment, sir." Then: "Transferring, sir."

After two rings, her voice: "Hello?"

Impulsively, I spoke in a really bad Brooklyn accent: "Yuh, this is the kitchen. Just double-checkin' an order for two cheeseburgers."

"I didn't order anything," she said.

"What? Youse didn't? Is this room one-two-six-six?"

"No," she said, "four-one-one-three."

"Oh, I'm sorry, ma'am. Someone musta messed up the ticket here. I'm really sorry."

"That's okay," she said. "But while you're at it, send up a bottle of Wild Turkey."

"Youse got it, lady." She bought the phony voice. Maybe I should've been an actor.

I called back, asked for room service. I ordered a bottle of Wild Turkey for room 4113.

I called Southwest Airlines. Their next flight to Las Vegas was in an hour and a half. I booked a seat on my MasterCard.

I took a quick shower, tossed some clothes in a bag, and drove to the airport.

The flight to Vegas took forty-five minutes.

The cab ride to the Stardust Hotel took twenty minutes.

I figured there'd be plenty of bourbon in that bottle when I got there.

I took the elevator to the fourth floor.

Room 4113. I knocked on the door.

Cassandra was wearing white slacks and a blue, see-through blouse, holding a glass of bourbon.

She looked me up and down. "Mr. Lansdale."

"Please," I said, pushing her aside and walking in. "After all we've been through, *Cassandra,* you can call me *Philip.*"

ood God," she said, and I could tell she was close to a good drunk, "you're the last face I expected to see when I opened the door."

"Did you expect Boyd Urick?" I asked, sitting on the bed. I looked around the room. "Nice room?"

"Boyd?" she said. "I wish."

"Uh-huh."

"I can't bloody believe you're here in Las Vegas."

"Believe it, baby."

"You're really pissing me off."

"Live with it."

"Did you come here thinking you'd fuck me?"

"That's the last thing I want from you," I said. She looked surprised. She started to pace.

"How did you know I was here?" she asked.

I told her about the caller ID, my phone call, my ordering her the bottle she had in her hand.

"Funny story," she said, sitting next to me.

"Aren't you going to offer me a drink?"

She handed me the bottle.

"I'm all ears."

"I like your ears."

"I'm listening," I said.

I didn't touch her. I had no desire to touch her. I wanted the truth, and she gave it to me.

She grew up in Sussex, the United Kingdom and had a sister, Beatrice. The summer of her seventeenth birthday, after she graduated high school, her parents thought it might be nice if she and her sister took a one-month trip somewhere. Beatrice wanted to go to the United States, so the U.S. it was. Cassandra just wanted to go somewhere. "I was a real wildcat," she said. "My first boyfriend, his name was Charles. He broke my heart. I wanted to marry him. He didn't want to marry me. He said it was impossible. Then he turns around and marries a rich girl."

She and Beatrice went to New York City first, staying at a moderately priced hotel. Beatrice entertained herself by going to plays and coffee houses and Cassandra picked up a small newspaper focusing on sexual fetishes. She saw ads for certain bars. When Cassandra was sure that Beatrice was asleep, she got into a short, tight skirt and a cut-off top and took a cab to one of these bars.

This is where she met Boyd Urick, and Boyd Urick was why she was in Las Vegas right now.

Boyd spotted Cassandra in the bar and made his move. He was slick, persuasive, but he didn't know Cassandra was easy and that her intention in coming here was the same as his: to find a sex partner for the night. They went back to his hotel room, which was shoddier than the one she was staying at. They smoked crack cocaine, which Boyd had a lot of, and had sex all night. Boyd didn't want her to go, and so she didn't. She forgot about her sister—she didn't care about her sister. All she wanted to do was get high and fuck Boyd.

He was from Las Vegas. She didn't know what he did, or why he was in New York. He seemed to have money and a lot of drugs.

Later—much later—she'd discovered what Boyd was doing in New York: he was moving counterfeit money for a third party. He delivered the fake bills to a buyer, who purchased it at fifty cents on the dollar, and Boyd delivered the real money to the printer of the fake money, taking a small cut for himself.

Cassandra liked Boyd, but it was Boyd who said he loved her. He said he loved her the moment he set eyes on her.

"No one had ever said they loved me," Cassandra told me, "so that was the magic key to my young, innocent heart."

Boyd suggested she go back to Las Vegas with him, live

with him, be his girlfriend and lover and wife. Cassandra didn't hesitate. She had nothing to return to. She could start anew in the US of A.

She sent a note to the hotel where Beatrice was. She knew her sister was probably very worried.

Don't worry, I'm safe, the note said. *I'm not going back home. I've met someone and we're in love and I'm staying in the States. I'll write home now and then. This is best for everyone.*

So began her new life.

"The first month in Vegas was heaven," Cassandra said. "Boyd had a nice one-bedroom apartment, he had money, and we had sex all the time. He took me out with him, I met his friends, they all knew what I was, and no one sneered or criticized.

"Boyd was a small-time crook, and it didn't take long for me to figure this out. He didn't have a real job. He ran the counterfeit bills, he dealt in stolen property, but mostly he gambled. He was a professional gambler. He was reasonably good at it, too, because he always had enough money for us to live on. While he'd make a big score now and then, most of it was lost when he tried to make an even bigger score, when he tried to 'break the bank' at the casinos. But I have to say, he at least was smart enough to put a third of every big win into the bank.

"I'd been living with him five months when he was arrested. He'd been in a stolen car with two other men. He called from jail and said his bail was fifty thousand dollars. 'Cassy-cass,' he said—he always called me that, 'Cassy-cass, go to the bank, withdraw five grand, and take it to this bail bondsman. He only needs ten percent. Do it now. Get me the fuck out of here!' "

She sighed. "So I went to the bank, got the money, and bailed him out. There had been seven thousand dollars in the bank, and now there was two.

"Boyd was facing a grand theft charge, and I was terrified he'd go to prison, but the district attorney dropped the charges not long after the arraignment. Something to do with a man whose car they'd stolen—a criminal himself—and that the cops who'd arrested them screwed up the facts in their reports.

"Boyd and his friends had a huge party to celebrate their exoneration. It was that night, very high on coke, that Boyd talked me into having sex with him and a friend.

"I felt very dirty the next day, believe it or not."

"I don't," I said.

She took the bottle from me. "Well, I did. Anyway, Boyd started going downhill after that. He began losing more than winning, drinking more. He also started hitting me. It was horrible.

"He was arrested again. Two detectives came to the door one morning to take him in. He nodded and complied. The detectives looked at me and one shook his head.

"There wasn't enough money in the bank to bail him out this time, and the charges, he told me, would probably stick. 'What I did was stupid,' he said, 'and I have to do some time for it.' He got a year in county jail."

"What did he do?" I asked.

"I have no idea. He wouldn't tell me. I didn't want to know." She drank, and went on with her story:

Alone now and she didn't know what to do. There was twelve hundred in the bank. Boyd told her to put two hundred on his jail books, so he could buy candy bars and sodas, and to keep the thousand to live on. A thousand wasn't going to last, she knew this. She waited until the end of the month, moved out of the apartment and into a cheap studio.

The move left her with four hundred dollars. She would need to find a job. She had no idea how she would do that. It occurred to her that she would have to have sex for money.

She met Lawrence Payne at a hotel bar.

Lawrence Payne heard her order a whiskey sour from the

bar, piqued by her accent. He was drinking a beer. "Hello," he said.

She, too, was startled by that familiar accent, an accent she hadn't heard in almost a year. Since her stay in America, she hadn't once crossed paths with a fellow British citizen.

"Liverpool?" he said.

"Sussex," she said.

"London, myself."

"You live in London?"

"I live in California."

He was a handsome older man in his mid-forties; she was attracted to him and Cassandra knew he felt the same way, or maybe they just both liked hearing a familiar accent. He offered to buy her another drink and she accepted and then there was a third drink, a fourth, a fifth. He was drunker than she, and starting to be a bit more bold—touching her hand as they talked. She didn't remember what they talked about and it probably wasn't important. He did tell her that he'd been married before, divorced for almost seven years, and he had no one in his life. He mentioned he had a room in this hotel and she suggested they go there and order some room service, so they did.

She wasn't going to ask him for money. She liked him too much to do this.

Once in the room, he wanted to kiss her. She kissed him. They ordered room service—more alcohol, some food. Lawrence Payne was more interested in kissing her and touching her. She let him remove her blouse, but not her bra. Every time he tried to put his hand between her legs, she would stop him.

Finally, after the fourth or fifth time she blocked that wandering hand, he said, "If you're afraid I'll find a penis, I already know it's there."

"What?" I said.

Cassandra smiled at me.

I stood up. I looked down at her. She kept smiling and then stopped.

"You didn't know?" she said.

"What?" I said again.

"Oh come on, Philip," she said, "I used to be a man."

I sat down on the chair.

"You didn't know?" she asked.

After everything that had happened to me, how could I be surprised by anything? She could have told me she was an alien from another dimension and it wouldn't have fazed me. Yeah, I was numb and in denial, here looking for order, for vengeance. I had thrown my life away for this woman, and she wasn't even a woman. It was par for the course. I deserved this. I deserved every fucking bit of this.

"Give me that bottle," I said.

Cassandra handed it over.

I drank. "But you don't have a dick."

"I had an operation," she said. I knew she was going to say that.

I didn't want to hear any more of her story, but she went on. "To cut to the chase, he was smitten with me. I spent the night with him. I left, but I came back the next night. He was happy to see me. I told him I wanted money for the sex and he laughed. I told him about my predicament. He suggested I come to California and live with him, so I did. Just like that, story of my life—I meet a man, the next thing I know I'm sharing a life with him. I counted my lucky stars, because Lawrence had money, being a banker, and being quite prudent with investments. But I didn't love him."

"Then?" I said.

"Or now," she said. "I never loved him. I was fond of him. I cared for him. But I found I wanted him out of my life. He wouldn't let me go, and I needed a new life."

"So you killed him."

"I'll get to that."

"Jesus, you did kill him."

"Not quite," she said.

Despite her cool feelings toward Lawrence Payne, and the fact that she was using him for security, he fell deeply in love with her, or so he said. He gave Cassandra the financial security she desperately needed, at which time she started thinking about having a sex change.

Their one-year anniversary—of the day they had met—Cassandra was nineteen and Lawrence said he'd give her whatever her heart desired as a gift. She said, "I want a sex change." He nodded, figuring that would be her request, and informed her that he'd looked into the matter, and that he did indeed have enough funds in an account in the Cayman Islands to give her this gift.

It was done in Switzerland.

She was made a woman.

They were married in Switzerland, too.

"For two years, we played the game of domesticated husband and wife very well," she said. "Our sex life was a normal one, but I suspected Lawrence missed the old me, in a way.

"It was building up, it was only a matter of time that I'd break my fidelity with Lawrence. I was proud of my cunt and wanted to put it to some good use. It happened, first, with a business associate of my husband's, and next with a stranger I chanced to meet in a bar. I started meeting more strangers. It started to become a habit, a very addictive habit, picking up strangers, mostly in hotel and airport bars. Lawrence being away a lot gave me much freedom.

"You were watching me, spying on me," she said, "you noticed I left the house and returned at all kinds of hours."

"Dressed to kill," I said.

"I was on the prowl for men," she said.

"Was I just another one? Am I?" I said. "Another man to fool?"

"Yes," she said plainly.

As I allowed that to sink in, she watched me, and continued.

"I didn't want to be married to Lawrence anymore. There was another life out there, I'm in my twenties and Lawrence was closing in on fifty and I *didn't* want to be a suburban American housewife. I told Lawrence this, but he refused to grant me a divorce.

"I started to think about Boyd Urick and what had happened to him, how he was doing. I made some calls to old acquaintances in Las Vegas, and was given his number.

"Boyd was ecstatic when he received my call. He thought I'd gone back to England.

" 'No,' I said, 'I'm a housewife in San Diego.'

" 'You're bullshitting me.'

" 'I'm not.'

"He wanted to see me. I told him to come in two days, and take a room, and I'd meet him there. Our hello embrace turned into a long kiss, and then we were on the bed, and it was almost like it had been years ago, the two of them making their own little universe in Las Vegas. But before it got to sex, I stopped him and said, 'Boydy-boyd, I'm different.' That's what I always called him: 'Boydy-boyd.'

"I took his hand and put it between my legs. I thought he'd be rollicking; instead his face paled and he cried, 'You mutilated yourself!'

"I thought he'd be pleased, that he would understand. He always knew I wanted the operation.

"He jumped away from me. He was upset. He wanted to know why a beautiful person as I would want to do such a thing. He said I'd done the wrong thing. I began to cry. He held me and told me he was sorry. He said he loved me, had always loved me, and wished I hadn't changed. 'People change,' I said.

"I wept and told him I didn't want to be married to Lawrence any longer. Boyd suddenly became all business. He said, 'Hubby is rich, right?' He questioned me about accounts, stocks, overseas investments, insurance. I told him what I knew. He was calculating it all in his head. He said if Lawrence were to be out of my life forever, I'd have well over three million to my name. Maybe more.

"I knew what he was getting at. I told him he was crazy. He said of course he was crazy, he always had been."

"Getting at?" I said. "Getting at what?"

"About having Lawrence killed," she said. She questioned him for hours. What were the logistics? What were the risks of her being arrested? How did she know the contractee wouldn't just take the money and run?

"We're talking *professionals* here," Boyd said. "These professionals always do the job. They have a code of honor, they live in a different world than you and I. They take one-third up front, and the other two-thirds when the job is done. These hit men live by a fucking code of honor. They have this crazy subculture all their own. They have their own morals and laws. But once you hire them, there's no turning back. There's no changing your mind. Even if you do change your mind—they still want the money. A deal is a deal with these folks."

"And you know these men?" she asked.

"Sometimes they're women," Boyd said. "I don't know any personally, but I know people who know how to get in contact with them."

"How much would it cost?"

"Let me ask around."

Two days later, he called and said, "Thirty grand, and it *can* be done."

"I can't come up with that kind of money," she said.

"I bet you can come up with the ten grand as down payment," Boyd said. "Then after he's dead, you'd have access to all his money, and can easily come up with the rest."

In fact, she *could* get her hands on ten thousand dollars. She took it out of three different accounts, because anything over ten thousand would be reported by the bank. She gave the money to Boyd to give to the person he knew who would give it to the contract killer. Cassandra didn't know when the hit would take place, she was told it'd happen within two weeks. It was best, Boyd informed her, that she knew as little as possible, for her own protection. She didn't know it was going to happen right after he left the airport. She was with Boyd that evening; she went to see him at a motel room, and he was in an especially good, sexual mood. (So this is who she went to see.) She should've known that he was well aware of the fact that as she was fucking him, her husband, and a cab driver, were having bullets pumped into their bodies.

But that wasn't the case. Boyd was as ignorant as she was regarding when and how the hit would take place.

When the police came to her house, she was shocked, so her act wasn't phony. Further, she was furious that someone else was killed. She never wanted anyone *else* to get hurt. Boyd told her these things happened. She was angry at him. The job, she felt, was sloppy, and she was afraid. He told her it was all right, and that the killer needed to be paid.

I said, "I saw Boyd visit you twice. Once, he spent the night. The second time, it was brief, and you were having an argument."

She nodded. "Yes, first he came over to collect the twenty thousand, plus five thousand as his personal fee. I was upset, and I let him stay with me. I just needed him to hold me, and he did. The second time, he wanted me to leave with him. I told him I didn't want to be with him. I told him that I was still angry that the innocent cab driver was killed."

Just as she thought she was in the clear, Detective Roger paid her a visit and started asking her curious questions: Did she know of any enemies Lawrence may have had? Was she sure she didn't leave the house the night her husband was killed? Had the insurance company paid off the policy yet? She was nervous. She knew the cop suspected something. She decided to do what she did best: seduce him. She gave him a few drinks, put on the charm, got close to him, and he was easily caught in her web. Now, if he did come up with anything on her, she would have the fact that he fucked her—and he was a married man—to mar any further investigation.

"Where do I fit in?" I asked.

"You don't," she said. "I happened to catch you peeping on me, and had a little fun with you."

"Do you know what has happened to my life? Because of all this?"

"I'm sorry about Jessica, and I'm sorry about Mr. Vaughn. I really am. But I am not at fault."

"You don't see the big picture, do you? The cause and effect."

"I have greater things to worry about, Mr. La—Philip. My life is in danger. The problem, the big problem, is that Boyd never delivered the twenty thousand to the hit man. I had no idea. I thought that was done and taken care of.

"Several days ago I received a call from a man with a deep, serious voice. He said he wanted his money. He said, 'You hired me to do a job, even though you turned around and hired someone else to take care of the matter, no arrangements were made with me. I planned the hit out, and learned the target was already eliminated. You still owe me the money we agreed on. We have a contract between us, you and I.'

"I realized who he was.

" 'We had an arrangement,' he said on the phone.

"I said that I gave Boyd the money, all of it.

" 'He didn't give it to me. Boyd has disappeared,' the man said on the phone.

" 'I gave him the money!' I cried.

"I started putting it together—Boyd must've paid someone else less money to kill Lawrence. Either way, the man on the phone wanted to be paid, and he was dead serious about it. I even said this to him. I said, 'You didn't do the job, why do you think you should get any money?'

" 'Because a contract was signed,' he said, very coldly.

"I suppose I could've come up with twenty grand, but I was scared," she said. "He said we'd meet. I knew that a person in his profession wouldn't risk me seeing him. I had the gut feeling that he'd take the money and kill me anyway, just for causing him trouble. And Boyd! That fucking bastard. He took the money for himself. That—turkey! The day the man called was the day you came over and the day your house caught on fire and your daughter . . ." She sighed. "There was just too much happening. I knew I had to leave, fast. I had to find Boyd and get my money back so I could pay the hit man off.

"And find out who really killed my husband."

17

Ho do you know Boyd is here? He could've gone any-where with that money."

"No," Cassandra shook her head. "Las Vegas is his air. He couldn't live without this city. I know what went through his mind. Boyd is a swindler and a little crook, and he wasn't happy with me, but I knew he would never wish me harm. Because he had to know the hit man would come after me.

"You see, this is what Boyd was thinking: he has twenty-thousand American dollars, he doesn't have to give it to the hit man right away, he has an opportunity to perhaps double the twenty to forty by gambling big, and making a better profit for himself."

"He has twenty-five really," I said. "The five you gave him."

She nodded. "That's right."

"So you believe he's gambling right now?"

"I believe he botched his plan. He lost more than he ex-pected. So he's trying to get it back. Because I'm certain that the hit man would not only want to kill me for not paying, but Boyd as well. Boyd knows this. And Boyd can't stay in Vegas unless he pays off the hit man. Therefore, I know Boyd is desperately scheming another way to 'break the bank' at some casino for the twenty thousand. You don't know how the gambler's mind works, Philip. I do, having lived with one for so long. He believes the Big Win is always around the corner and all his worries will be over. The Big Win is the Ultimate High, the ultimate laugh in the face of chance. But in Vegas, that never happens. Men like Boyd always get sucked in. Let them win a few small big ones, and believe they'll get the Big One . . . but instead, the casinos always wind up with your money. Gamblers are *sick* people. They're always trying to grab what they don't deserve."

"I think I understand a gambler's mind," I said, softly.

We sat there.

"That's my story"—she stood up—"What's yours?"

I stayed in my chair. "You know mine."

"I want more details."

"There aren't any. Have you tried looking for Boyd?" I asked.

"Last night. He only gambles at night, into the wee hours. Obviously I didn't find him."

"So let's go find him."

"Who is this 'we'?"

"You and I."

She said, "You should go back home."

"Home?" I said. "Home?" I stood up, facing her. "I don't *have* a fucking home! My daughter is *dead* and my wife has left me and I don't have a fucking *job* because I'm a fucking screwup, worse than Boyd. I have an *interest* in finding Boyd too! It's his fault that Bryan, about my only friend in the world, is in the hospital. Besides, you may need backup."

She thought about this. "Suit yourself. I suppose I could use the company."

"Say we do find him," I said, "then what? I don't think he'll be very cooperative."

"No, probably not." Cassandra opened a suitcase that was on the floor and reached in. "This will help him to cooperate." She was holding a silver-plated revolver.

"Where the hell did you get that?"

"Lawrence had it hidden in the house."

"Is it loaded?"

"Yes. Six bullets. This is called a thirty-eight."

"How did you get that on the plane?"

She gave me a look. "I drove here."

"Do you know how to use it?" I asked.

"Lord, no," she said. "I don't plan to *use* it. Just to scare Boyd. But if I have to use it . . . I just click off the safety, cock the hammer, and start firing. I feel safer with it. I might run into the hit man."

"Oh boy," I said.

"It's getting late," she said. "We should go hunt us a Boyd Urick."

I wish I could say that we found him in the first casino we looked in, but these things never happen. I was not confident we'd ever find him in the hundreds, if not thousands, of casinos in Las Vegas. Cassandra didn't feel this would be a problem. Boyd was a creature of habit, and there were only about two dozen places he liked to go to—or was allowed to go into. It would be a matter of frequenting each of them on a rotating basis, and keeping an eye out for him.

She inquired of some of the dealers and pit bosses at the casinos if they'd seen someone fitting Boyd's description recently. Some didn't bother with her, shrugging or shaking their heads with disinterest, and others—much to my surprise—knew who Boyd Urick was. She received answers ranging from Boyd not having been there in a while, to having been in last night. This reassured Cassandra that he was indeed in Las Vegas. I availed myself of the free drinks in the casinos, but the booze didn't sit well with me.

How could I be here in Vegas with all the tragedy I'd left behind in San Diego? It was easier than you think. It was easy to push it out of my head and forget it ever happened, and concentrate on assisting Cassandra in her search. I hated the fact that it was so easy.

I don't know what good or help I was, following her around, grabbing free drinks, putting a few quarters in the slot machines when the urge struck.

In one place, I got lucky. I came up three peaches, the machine honked at me, and poured out dozens of quarters. Quarters were falling to the ground. I tried to catch them all.

Cassandra laughed and said, "Don't let it seduce you."

Filling my pockets with quarters, I knew how it could.

A little old lady aggressively pushed me aside and said, "This machine is mine now!"

I felt silly sloshing around with pockets full of quarters, but by the end of the night—or morning—I would lose them all to other slot machines.

I was exhausted. Cassandra was getting tired, too. It was 4 A.M. We'd been to most of Boyd's favorite haunts at least three times. Cassandra was convinced we probably just missed him a few times, because that was the way this city worked.

"Time to turn in," she said.

"Thank God," I said.

"Where are you staying?"

"What do you mean?"

"I mean, where are you sleeping?"

"Well, I thought—"

"Oh, you *thought*," she said, giving me a sour look. "You thought, since we messed around a few times, that I would just open my bed up to you, to sleep together like we were lovers?"

"Well," I said. "Yes."

"You didn't take it well," she said. "Finding out the truth."

"I don't care anymore."

"You're very presumptuous."

"If we're not lovers, what are we?"

"We're neighbors."

"I'll get a room," I said.

"Oh bollocks, come on," and she took my arm.

In her room, she told me I could sleep in the bed with her, but to stay on my side. She didn't want to cuddle, kiss, and she especially didn't want to fuck. I thought it was somewhat cruel of her to then undress in front of me and get into bed naked after laying down these rules. But I found that I was unaroused seeing her body, or being in bed with her. I was just tired. The minute I closed my eyes, I was asleep.

18

Cassandra informed me I snored, but made light of this. We both woke up well into the afternoon. She told me to order up some food while she showered. I ordered plenty, and we ate. She was surprised I didn't order any booze and I told her I was thinking about quitting.

"I love alcohol too much to ever quit," she said. "I just hope I don't become an alcoholic." With that, she poured herself a glass of Wild Turkey from what was left of the bottle we had last night.

We finally found Boyd Urick in the first casino we walked into. "There he is." Cassandra stopped me with a hand to my chest and pointed to a thin man with long hair and a goatee at a blackjack table. It was him all right.

"So what do we do now?" I said.

"We don't want to cause a scene in here. We'll wait for him to leave."

We sat at the bar, where we could watch him. Cassandra had her usual Wild Turkey on the rocks, and I had a glass of water. Boyd was at the blackjack table for about half an hour; then got up and started toward the exit.

"He never stays put too long," she said. "Come!"

Outside, she said, "Boydy-boyd, you bastard, stop there."

He stopped. He turned. His jaw was agape.

"Cassy-cass," he said.

"Shocked to see me?" She moved close to him, as if for a hug. He seemed to start to hug her, until he felt the .38 in his side. "This is a gun, Boyd," she said, "you know about *guns*."

"Where'd you get a gun, Cassy-cass?" he said, trying to act amused. I could see that he was scared.

"Where's the money, Boydy-boyd?" she said.

He looked at me. "Who's this guy? Another freak like your dear departed husband?"

"This is Philip Lansdale, he's my neighbor," she said.

"Hi, Boyd," I said.

"Let's take a bit of a stroll, eh, Boydy-boyd?" she said.

We started walking.

"You didn't pay the hit man," she went on, "and now he wants to kill me."

"I had a plan, Cassy-cass, I wasn't going to fuck you over, I had a real good plan," and he explained to her his scheme to double the money, just as she'd told me that was what he was up to.

"But it didn't work, did it, Boydy-boyd? You didn't win."

"I was close, Cassy-cass."

"I've heard it before, honey."

"I was!"

"Too many times."

"*But I can feel it this time.*" He sounded pathetic. I wanted to smack him around.

"How much is left?" she asked.

"About ten grand."

"This is what we'll do," she said. "We'll go get that ten grand. I'll then get another ten from the bank, and you'll get in touch with this hit man, and I'm going to pay him off."

"Or what?" he said. "You'll shoot me?"

"*Where's* the money, Boydy-boyd?"

"In my motel room," he said.

"What? You don't have a place of your own?"

"I have a place," he said, "but I doubt it's safe. I'm sure Rook is looking for me, too."

"Rook is the hit man?"

"Yeah."

"You did his job, and now he's mad."

"I didn't do anything. I didn't kill anyone."

"You hired a cheaper hit man?"

"I thought Rook had done it," he said. "Then Rook tells me he didn't do it. I didn't know who did it. 'The wife hired someone else,' he said."

"No," Cassandra said, "I didn't."

"*Someone* offed your husband," Boyd said.

Cassandra became very quiet.

We walked down the strip to the motel room. It was a few blocks away. It was a ratty, dirty-looking place. How could a man leave ten grand unattended? Either Boyd knew something I didn't, or he was just stupid.

He opened the door and we went in.

"Well," a deep voice said, "home at last. And with company. The *very* woman I wanted to see."

Standing in the room was the large bald black man in the trench coat, holding the gun with a silencer, the same one he'd shot Bryan with. Also in the room was a platinum blonde with five-inch platforms, neon green stretch pants, and a bikini top barely covering her breasts. She also held a gun with a silencer. She was chewing gum.

She popped the gum, like a small gun shot.

19

Y ou must be Rook," Cassandra said.
"That's me," he said. "Drop your piece."
Cassandra didn't.
"Do it, bitch!" the platinum blonde girl said, blowing a bubble and popping it.
"This is Lucy," Rook said.
"Heya," Lucy smiled. "Now *drop the gun*, cuntdrip."
Cassandra let go of the .38.
"I was going to call you," Boyd said, nervously looking at two canvas bags on the bed.
"Sure you were, you little fucking liar." Rook aimed down and fired, shooting Boyd in the foot. Boyd screamed and fell, his foot spurting blood. "Now the game's a-foot!" He roared with laughter, and so did Lucy.
I felt like I was going to be sick. The room started to spin. I told myself that this horrible thing wasn't happening. It couldn't be. I was home, asleep and dreaming.
Rook turned the gun on Cassandra. "Where do you want it? Where would a bullet do you most good?"
"Look," Cassandra said coolly, "it's not my fault this turkey didn't pay you the balance. I had no idea he took off with the money."
"*I was going to pay you, Rook!*" Boyd screamed.
"When?" said Rook. "When you damn well *pleased?*"
"*Today!*"
"Sheeet."
"Kill him," Lucy said. "Just kill him. I don't like him." She popped her gum.
"Please don't kill him," Cassandra said.
I almost fell down, my head was so light. I leaned against

the wall. Rook pointed his gun at me. He asked, "And just who the heck is this?"

"No one involved," Cassandra told him, "he's a friend."

"I *know* you, friend," he said to me.

I shook my head.

He stepped closer, examining my face. "I'll *be*. The other day in San Diego. You were across the street, when I shot that fat old fart with the mouth."

"He was—" I said, but then couldn't speak.

"What is it? You here to avenge him? Nosy people come to messy ends, *friend*."

"He's the friendly neighbor," Boyd snickered.

"Shut the fuck up," Lucy said, kicking Boyd in the chest. Boyd grunted, curling in on himself. "Rook, let's kill him and get out of here," Lucy said. She was impatient.

"I didn't plan on there being company," Rook said. "We now have three bodies to contend with."

"Mr. Rook," Cassandra said.

"It's just 'Rook,' cunthole," Lucy said.

Cassandra said, "There's ten thousand here. I can get the other ten from my bank account in the morning. You'll be paid, and I hope that you'll accept my apology, and there will be no reason to go to such extremes."

"That's awfully nice of you," Rook said, and he did seem touched. "It's not that easy. Business protocol was fucked with, and it's bad business just to let it go. You hire me, then you hire someone else. Baaaaad. Now, I was pleased to come in here and find exactly ten thousand and fifty-three dollars." He opened one of the canvas bags, and grinned. "But lo and behold, much to my great stupefaction, look what else I found." He opened the other bag, turned it upside down, and emptied the contents on the bed: several dozen bundles of twenties and hundreds. "Fifty grand, if I'm not mistaken."

"It's funny money," Boyd said, his voice barely above a squeak.

"That's what I thought. But funny money can be sold. So let's say I take the ten g's, and the fifty in funny g's, kill the three of you, and we'll call this misunderstanding settled."

"That's the Krabava's money," Boyd said, spit flying from his mouth, his foot still bleeding profusely on the carpet.

"What do I give a fuck about the Krabava syndicate?" Rook said. "I never worked for them, and I don't expect them to ever hire me. Motherfucking Russians. Come in and take over, the Italians go over to Wall Street. This world is coming to an end."

"I'm responsible for that money," Boyd said, almost crying. "Do you know what they'll *do* to me?"

"What? Kill you?" Rook laughed, pointed the gun, and shot Boyd in the middle of the eyes. The hole was neat. Boyd's body fell back on the floor, and I didn't doubt for a second that he was quite dead. "Now you don't have to worry about them killing you, Boyd."

"Oh, Boydy-boyd," Cassandra said. She was doing a good job of maintaining, but I could see her skin start to crawl, her body start to shake.

"It was going to happen sooner or later," Rook said. "Damn thing is, I kinda liked the little loser. He talked about you a lot, Cassandra Payne. You know what he told me. He said you have a dick."

"He said she *used* to have a dick," Lucy said.

"Oh yeah. Used to. Is that right? Did you used to be a chick with a dick?"

"That's so per*verse*," Lucy said, popping gum, "that's so *unnatural*."

"Is it true," Rook said, "or do I have to cop a feel?"

"Don't you touch that thing!" Lucy shrieked.

"It's true," Cassandra said.

"I'll *be*," Rook said. "You know, I met you and didn't know, I wouldn't know. I'd say you're a woman."

"I am a woman," Cassandra said.

"*I'd* know," Lucy said. "*I* can spot a transo anywhere anytime, post- or preop."

"Listen to me, Rook," Cassandra said. "There's no reason to hurt me. You have your money. I had every intention of paying you off. I had no idea someone else did the hit. And there's no reason to hurt Mr. Lansdale," she added, looking at me, "he has nothing to do with this."

"Can we kill them *now?*" Lucy said. "I *really* want to kill this former chick with a dick *now.*"

"Wait," Rook said.

"Wait!"

"I'm having," and he took a deep breath, "a moral dilemma."

"*Fuck* that! They both saw you kill Boyd, and him," she said, pointing her gun at me, "he saw you off that guy in San Diego."

"He's not dead," I said.

"Really," Rook said, "he survived three close slugs?"

"He's in the hospital."

"Must be a tough old fart."

"He is," I said.

"Rook," Lucy said.

"*Quiet!*" he told her.

She pouted.

"I understand that Boyd screwed up and it wasn't your fault," Rook told Cassandra, "but do you understand my position?"

"Yes," she said, "I do."

"I don't think so," Rook said. "You're just saying that. You're just trying to butter me up."

"I understand that you take your profession seriously," Cassandra said, "and that any breach, no matter who is at fault, must be dealt with on all sides . . . the go-between, and the person who put out the contract. It sends a message: that you are not a man to be screwed with."

"Don't listen to her," Lucy said.

"Maybe you do understand," Rook said. "It hurts me when there's no trust in me to get the job done."

"I trusted what Boyd told me," Cassandra said. "I'm sure you would've pulled off the job with excellence."

"The way it was done, it was so messy and amateurish," Rook said. "The cab driver. I would've *never* done that."

Lucy looked like she was getting irritated. She put her gun to Cassandra's temple. "Say so long to your brains, Ms. Post-op."

Rook took the gun from Lucy. "No."

"Rook, you nuts?"

"I'm confused about what to do. I told you—"

"Yeah, yeah, your moral dilemma."

Rook looked at Cassandra, then at me, then at Boyd's dead body. He began to zip up the canvas bags of money.

"There's only one thing to do," he said, "take this to the Arbiter."

"Oh, God," Lucy moaned, "not him."

"Yeah, I gotta. I just gotta."

I wanted to be back home more than anything right now.

Cassandra and I sat in the back of Rook's black vintage Mustang. Lucy, in the passenger seat, turned to face us, gun in hand. She really looked like she wanted to shoot. The moment we'd gotten into the car, Rook had put a tape in the tape deck, and Creedence Clearwater Revival began their version of "Suzy-Q." Rook had a good sound system, the bass throbbing, the guitar screeching, the drums pounding.

We drove out of the strip for about two miles, closing in on the desert. Rook pulled into what looked like an abandoned casino.

It was a show, and we were the only four people in a theater that had at least two hundred seats. Big band music played, but there was no band, it was coming out of hidden speakers. Lights came on. The red curtains on the stage parted, and two strippers were on each side, left and right, in sequins and G-strings, feathered wigs and boas and glitter. They began to move sensually about the poles as the big-band music segued into an instrumental version of "I've Got You Under My Skin." A follow spot came onto an electric wheelchair. In the wheelchair was a white-haired man without legs; his skin was pale and he wore large, Elvis-like glasses and a blue, gold-sequined jacket. He also held a black gavel in his hand. He didn't have anything to pound the gavel on, he just waved it about. He took center stage as the women continued to dance and the music faded.

"I am the Arbiter," said the man in the wheelchair with no legs. "Who has summoned this court into session?"

Rook stood, seemingly humble. "I have."

"And who are you?"

"They call me Rook, sir."

"Yes, Rook. You've been here several times before. What can I help you with?"

"Arbiter, I have a moral dilemma."

"A quandary?"

"A real pickle."

"Give it to me in a nutshell."

Rook explained. "I was hired to take out a woman's husband for thirty grand, this woman here," indicating Cassandra, "although she used to not be a woman, but that's a whole bird of a different color. I was given the down payment of ten grand, I planned out the job, I went to do it, only to discover that the target was already taken care of. Another player was in the game. I was never taken off the job, I was never informed—not only was my good name smeared, I wasn't paid the balance, as was my right.

"I guess it wasn't the woman's fault, the cardplayer took off with the money, but I found them together in a motel room, along with this other man," indicating me, "which complicates matters. I wasn't sure what was going on. Were they all in cahoots? I killed the cardplayer for having cheated me."

"As was your right," said the Arbiter.

"I was going to kill the wife and the man, but I started to think . . . She had no idea I wasn't paid. She seemed to have come to Vegas to right the wrong caused by the cardplayer. I was going to kill them, but . . ."

"You're worried about karma?"

"Yes, sir."

"Where is the woman, this wife?"

Lights flashed on us. I covered my eyes.

The man in the wheelchair pointed his gavel. "Are you the woman who made the contract?"

"Yes," Cassandra said.

"Did you know Rook had not been paid the balance?"

"No. Not at first."

"Why did you come to Las Vegas?"

"To find B—the cardplayer Rook mentioned. He stole the money. I wanted to get it back, and pay Rook. I was afraid Rook might come after me and kill me."

"Which I did," Rook said, "but she wasn't home, and I shot someone else, but he was putting his nose in my business. Which could get me in danger. No bad karma there."

"But you had no ill intentions to cheat Rook out of his money?" the Arbiter said.

"No," Cassandra said.

"Rook, has the account been settled?" the Arbiter asked.

Rook said, "That's the dilemma, sir. The cardplayer had half the money, which was ten grand. But he had fifty g's in funny money, which is worth a good twenty or more."

"Ah! So you come out better because of all this!"

"Yes, sir."

"So, why kill these two?"

"Well, they witnessed me kill the cardplayer."

"But it was in your right to kill the cardplayer for cheating you."

"It was—"

"But the woman had no intention of cheating you."

"No—"

"And you made more money than you originally planned."

"Yeah—"

"Then it would be bad karma if you killed her and the man she is with."

"I was afraid of that."

"Let them live," the legless man in the wheelchair said, and the music started up again, and the strippers began to dance.

I leaned into Cassandra and asked, "What the *hell* is this?"

"You know," she replied in a whisper, "Las Vegas. *Everything* is a show."

Not to mention surreal. At that very moment, five men in suits and ties burst in, brandishing guns, holding out badges, yelling, "*Freeze! United States Treasury Department!*" No one froze and bullets started to fly. It all happened so fast. Rook and Lucy were shooting. The two strippers suddenly had guns—I don't know where they were keeping them—and shooting. Even the legless man had a gun and was shooting. Bullets were flying everywhere. This firepower took the men in suits by surprise and they were all shot down. One of the strippers was shot in the face. The air was filled with cobalt discharge. I looked at all the blood and gore and thought, there's too much senseless violence in the world.

"Holy shit," Rook said, when it was over.

"Who are they?" Lucy said, her legs shaking.

I noticed, then, that Cassandra was holding onto me, tight, and she was shaking, too.

I was numb.

The surviving stripper left the stage, took the badge and ID off a slain man, and brought it to the Arbiter.

The air was thick with something.

The Arbiter made a face. "T-Men! Rook, this is your doing! Goddamn T-Men!"

"I don't understated," Rook said. He looked very worried, something that didn't quite fit his demeanor.

"What's there not to understand?" said the Arbiter. "You're carrying around a large sum of counterfeit money. You attracted the attention of Treasury agents."

"Fucking card player," Rook said under his breath.

"Yes. They must've been on his tail. Waiting for the exchange. Instead, you kill him and take off with the funny money."

"*Shit!*" Rook kicked a seat.

"You've really inconvenienced me, Rook. We have to clear out of here fast before more Feds show their faces." The Arbiter groaned. "Do you know what this *means*? I have to find a new theater."

Rook hung his head down. "I'm sorry, sir." He sounded like he really meant it.

"You'll pay for this later, Rook."

"Yes, sir."

"Now we have a problem on our hands, Rook. Another moral question."

"Sir?"

"Those two," pointing at me and Cassandra.

"I'm sick of these two," Lucy said. "I really am! We should've never brought them here! Rook, we should've killed them like I said!"

"Girl," said the Arbiter, "shut the fuck up."

Lucy was about to reply, and Rook smacked her across the head.

"Owie," Lucy said.

Rook glared at her. She looked away.

"*Who* is she?" asked the Arbiter.

"My girlfriend, Lucy," Rook said.

"You need to teach the bitch some manners."

"I will, sir."

"I changed my mandate," said the Arbiter. "Take those two," pointing at Cassandra and me, "and kill them."

"But . . ."

"*But?*"

"I was told a mandate can never be changed."

"Mitigating circumstances. We just offed a bunch of Feds. Survival can change a mandate. I can change my own goddamn mandates any way I please."

"What about karma?"

"Self-preservation comes before karma. You will have to deal with the karma when the time comes." He pointed a finger. "Do you, Rook, have the audacity to go against me?"

Rook shook his head. "No, sir, no."

"Well, go bury them deep out in the desert where no one will ever find them."

"Yes sir!"

20

Back in the Mustang, Lucy holding the gun on us, Rook driving, "Suzy-Q" blaring out the speakers. The hellish part was that the song kept playing over and over. Either Rook had a tape that endlessly looped, or the song had been recorded several times. We were heading north, far from Las Vegas, it was past one in the morning. Rook must've been going eighty or ninety. I was holding Cassandra's hand.

"Rook," Cassandra said.

He didn't hear her.

"Rook!"

He turned the volume of the music down. "Yeah?"

"You don't have to kill us," she said. "You can let us off. We won't say anything. You know we won't."

"Yeah. But I gotta."

"The Arbiter said—"

"He said he changed his mind and to bury you."

"But you don't have to do what he says. He's not your boss."

Rook shook his head. "No way. Bad mojo you go against what the Arbiter says. You just don't do that."

Finally, I said something. I said, "Who made him God?"

Rook said, "The Arbiter has paid his dues, he's seen it all, done it all."

"He doesn't even have any legs!" I screamed.

"Lost them on a hit," Rook said. "Still, he got the job done. Don't worry. We'll be swift, and bury you somewhere nice."

"I wanna shoot her soooooo bad," Lucy said, putting the gun against Cassandra's nose.

Rook turned the music back up.

We drove for what seemed like a long time. There was nothing but an endless stretch of highway, darkness, and stars.

Rook looked in the rearview and said, "Aw, crap."

"What?" said Lucy.

"Five-oh flagging us down."

Lucy said, "Oh, junk."

I turned my head, and so did Cassandra. Flashing red lights were coming in close.

Rook slowed down.

"This sucks," Lucy said.

"Keep cool," Rook said.

"It's about those Feds we killed."

"No. No. There'd be helicopters and a shitload of police cars. It's just a slap-happy Nye County sheriff. Put the gun down, Lucy. You two back there, keep calm, keep cool, and we'll get out of this without too much of a mess. Lucy, play it by ear."

"Right," she said, putting a new piece of gum in her mouth.

Rook pulled over and turned the music off. I was grateful just to have that song out of my life.

The cop, who was in fact a deputy sheriff, strolled up. He was your stereotypical out-in-the-middle-of-nowhere sheriff— beer belly and wide-brimmed hat, wearing shades even though it was the middle of the night. He flashed a light on all of us. Rook grinned as he rolled down the window.

"Howdy, officer."

"Son, you were driving way past the speed limit. Why you in such a hurry?"

Lucy brought the gun up and fired. Rook screamed, the gun going off near his face. The sheriff's own face turned into a bloody mess, spraying over Rook and the car.

"Goddammit, Lucy!" Rook cried. "I'm deaf now!"

"You're not deaf!"

"You don't shoot a gun in front of a man's face!"

"You said play it by ear!"

"Not *my* ear!"

"Is he dead?"

Rook looked down at the sheriff's body. "He looks pretty dead."

"That was close," Lucy said.

"Shit! My ears! Ringing!" He got out.

"You'll be okay." She turned to us. "He always has to make a big fuss about things." She made a face.

Lucy held the gun on us as Rook dragged the sheriff's body into the police cruiser, then he pushed the cruiser off the road and into the darkness. He got back in the car.

"Any day a cop dies is a good day. Okay," he said. "We get rid of these two, switch license plates, and lay low for a week in Arizona."

"Where we going in Arizona?" Lucy asked.

"I dunno. Phoenix."

"I fucking hate Phoenix."

"You never been to Phoenix."

"Yes I have and the place sucks."

"So where we gonna go?"

"Grand Canyon."

"Too many people."

"Sedona."

"Where's Sedona?"

"By Flagstaff."

"Why there?"

"I hear it's a wonderful and spiritual place."

"I could go for spiritual."

"You're a very spiritual guy, Rook. That's why I love you so much."

"Oh honey bunch!"

"Oh sweetums!"

They embraced and kissed. It was a very strange thing to watch.

"Okay," Rook said, putting the music back on, "we'll go there."

He started to drive. He hadn't bothered to clean the blood off himself or the car.

The two started to sing along with Creedence Clearwater Revival again. What may have explained their behavior came next. They began to smoke crack out of a pipe. I knew it was crack because they told me so. Rook offered us some. "Wanna smoke a few hits of rock?" he said. "It'll make everything easier."

"I is just a cwack hoe," Lucy laughed as she smoked from the pipe.

Cassandra whispered, "Take it easy, Philip."

How could I take anything easy in a situation like this? But surprisingly, I was. I was ready for anything, and knew I deserved what I had coming to me.

We drove for about twenty minutes.

Rook stopped the car. "This is as good a spot as any."

"Here?" Lucy said.

"Here."

"Time to get out," Lucy popped her bubble gum.

We got out. There was a strong wind. Rook left the headlights on, "Suzy-Q" still playing loudly.

"Go get the shovel out of the trunk," Rook said.

"You get it," Lucy said.

"Just get the damn shovel, girl."

She huffed, and opened the trunk. Rook had his gun on us. Lucy tossed the shovel to Rook. She had something else in her hand.

"What are you doing?" Rook said.

"My imitation of Cassandra here." I saw she had a long, black dildo. She stuck it between her legs and started chanting, "I'm a chick with a dick! I'm a chick with a dick!"

Rook roared with laughter.

Lucy jumped in front of Cassandra and waved the rubber phallus. Cassandra stared at the platinum blonde with disgust.

"Remind you of the old days?" Lucy said. "*I'm a chick with a dick!*"

"You're not amusing, little girl," Cassandra said.

"I'll show you amusing!" Lucy hit Cassandra in the face with the dildo and laughed. Rook laughed. Cassandra took the blow without a flinch. "Little girl my ass! *At least I am a girl!*"

"Okay," Rook said, "enough fun and games. Let's get this shit over with."

"*Finally*," Lucy said.

They marched us out into the pitch-black desert. I almost fell several times. The ground at my feet was full of holes, littered with unexpected large rocks.

In the distance behind us, all I could see was the car, its headlights, the faintness of that damn song playing over and over.

Above, thousands of stars. In another context, it would have been beautiful.

Rook, Lucy, and Cassandra were barely visible dark shapes.

I was going to be killed and murdered out in the middle of nowhere. I decided I deserved this. Every bit of it.

A light shined on us. First, it was a small flashlight—next, a larger, brighter one.

"Well, what do we have here?" an amused voice said.

21

More light flooded on us, the high beams of a truck. Rook and Lucy were dumbfounded. The two men holding shotguns didn't seem to be members of the human race. They were dirty, in mud-covered denim overalls, with greasy hair and missing teeth. They looked like they'd stepped right out of *Deliverance*, The wind whistled around us.

"Why don't you drop that gun, boy," one of them said to Rook.

"Why don't you suck my dick?" Rook retorted.

"Now, you might just be doin' that yo'self, badly," the other laughed.

"Rednecks!" Lucy spat her gum out. "I *fucking hate* rednecks! I ran away from home to get away from rednecks and *every*where I turn, you assholes *pop* up! There's no getting rid of you! You're like a *disease* on the rear end of humanity!"

"Whoooo, that mouth on this girl," one of the rednecks said.

"And look at this one here," said the other one, nodding at Cassandra.

"We gonna have us some *fun* tonight!"

"Whoooo-weeee!"

"What're you two yokels doing out here in the dark?" Rook said. "Blowing each other's peckerwoods?"

The rednecks laughed.

Lucy started to shoot. She got one redneck in the arm. The other blew a hole in her chest with his shotgun, and then he was killed by Rook: several *puff-puffs*, silenced bullets, in the chest and face. The one who'd gotten it in the arm shot out a gaping, bloody hole in Rook's chest. Rook just looked at the wound and said, "Aw, shucks." Music was still coming from the parked Mustang, an outlandish soundtrack to this madness.

I don't know what I wasn't thinking—*I wasn't thinking*. I was acting on instinct or impulse, the desire to live, or maybe I'd seen it in a movie. Like the Arbiter said, "self-preservation." I saw Lucy's gun next to her body and dove for it. I thought I heard Cassandra say, "No," but that could have been myself telling myself not to do it. But I did it. The injured redneck shot Rook again, and this time Rook went down. I was in the dirt, pointing the gun at the redneck, who smiled at me. I pulled the trigger—I kept pulling it, emptying every bullet into the redneck, the gun going *click-click-click*.

There was silence, except: *"Oh, Suzy-Q, baby I love you, Suzy-Q . . ."*

"Oh my goodness," Cassandra said.

I stood up and surveyed the carnage.

"Oh my goodness," Cassandra said again, her hand at her chest.

"Are you all right?" I said to her.

"My heart needs to slow down."

I dropped the gun.

Cassandra took the gun and wiped if off with her shirt, carefully placing it back next to Lucy.

"You don't want your prints on anything," she said.

"They're all dead."

"Of course they're *dead*, you goose."

"What do we do now?"

"We get the hell out of here. Come." She took my hand, and we quickly made our way back to the Mustang. Cassandra removed her shirt, standing in the cold night in a black bra; she popped open the trunk. She removed one of the canvas bags. "My money," she explained. "Wait," she said. "We best not take Rook's car. Every police agency in Nevada is probably looking for it. We'll take the Howdy-Doody boys' truck."

"Then what?"

"We go back to Vegas. We ditch the truck. We leave town."

I reached into the Mustang and yanked the tape out. Finally—*finally*—there was no music, but I knew it'd stay in my head for a long, long time.

"Thank you," she said.

"I used to like the song."

We walked back to the scene of the crime. Seeing all those bodies, all that blood and human flesh and bone, illuminated by the truck's high beams, I started to cry. It was overwhelming, and it struck me, really struck me, that my beautiful little daughter was dead, and it was my fault that she was dead, and because I couldn't keep a leash on my libido, a whole lot of people were now dead. I was drowning in a sea of dead bodies. I fell to my knees and bawled, thousands of stars twinkling high above. I screamed up at God. I wanted an explanation for all this. I wanted to believe that none of this had happened, that nothing like this could ever be real.

"Blimey, Mr. Lansdale," Cassandra Payne said, "get a grip on yourself."

She helped me to my feet.

"I don't know how to drive one of these big trucks," she said. "Do you?"

"Yeah."

"Good."

I forced myself to concentrate.

I got behind the wheel and she sat next to me. The cab smelled like fish and cigarette smoke. The floor was littered with empty beer cans, fast-food bags and wrappers.

"A couple of winners," I muttered, started the truck, put her in gear, and drove. I don't know if I was referring to the dead rednecks or us.

Silent, we went south, back toward Las Vegas. I could see a patch of lights miles ahead: the undeniable city.

"Something else is going to happen to us," I said.

"Think positively," she said.

"How much can happen to two people in one night?" I said.

"It's not over. Something bad is going to happen."

"We'll be *all right*," she said.

I imagined a blockade of police cars waiting for us. Or drunk tourists coming the other way, crashing into us. And why not? It'd all be part of this bizarre day, and would make sense.

We closed in on Vegas.

"Once we're in the city, I'll go to my room, pack, and leave," she told me.

"Where are we going?"

"I know where I'm going, and I'm not going to tell you. You should just go home and—"

"We're not leaving together?" I said.

"What gave you that idea?"

"I don't know."

"I never asked you to come here," she said. "I never asked you to help me find Boyd. I *didn't* ask you, I didn't force you. And there's nothing between us. We may have fooled around a couple of nights, Mr. Lansdale, but I don't like you."

"Gee, thanks," I said.

"I'm sorry, but I had to tell you. I have no romantic feelings for you, despite whatever you may feel. You weren't the only neighbor on the block I was messing around with, you know."

"What?"

"Don't act so dumbfounded," she said. "There was another, long before you came around. They always fall in love with me, when I tell them not to. Then they do damn fool things for that love."

She was quiet for a while.

"Every damn thing we do in life is for love," I said, feeling very small.

"It has only now occurred to me who killed my husband and the cab driver," she said. "Why didn't I figure it out before? He wanted Lawrence out of the picture, but I still wasn't going to see him. Or be with him. How could I? He's not my type."

"Who?" I asked.

"Like I'm really going to tell you," she said sarcastically.

She looked at me, like I should have known. I didn't know shit.

At the outskirts of the city, we parked the truck, wiped it for prints, and went to a pay phone. We called two cabs. We didn't speak as we waited. She held the canvas bag with real money, her shirt wrinkled and dirty. The cabs arrived.

"Well," I said.

"Cheerio," she said.

I told the cab driver to take me to the airport. It was four in the morning.

The first flight to San Diego left at five-fifty.

By seven-thirty, I was back home. Frankly, I didn't care who killed Lawrence Payne. Maybe he deserved it, for having married such a fucked-up individual like Cassandra. He deserved it like I deserved it.

The house was empty and lonely. I didn't want to be there. But here I was.

22

Not five minutes after I'd walked into my house, the doorbell rang. I expected anything—the police, a hit man friend of Rook's, perhaps Cassandra Payne herself. It was David.

"I saw you drive up," he said, coming inside. "Where have you been?"

"Here and there," I said.

"It's Bryan. He died last night in the hospital."

Another dead body. I sat down. I didn't know how to react. I guess I knew that Bryan was right—he wasn't going to make it. People were dying all around me and I was taking it in stride.

"Ellen's taking it pretty bad," David said.

I reminded myself of the promise I had made to Bryan.

"I went to see Cassandra," I told him.

"I know. I talked to her on the phone. She said you'd be coming back, and that you knew the truth."

"What do you mean you talked to her?"

"She called me."

"She—called you?"

"It's what she wanted!" he started blathering. "I thought I was doing her a favor. I thought . . . I thought . . . I thought she'd love me for it." He looked at me. "She told you everything?"

"No," I said. I started putting it together. The way he acted the day at my barbecue . . .

"You were fucking her, too?" he said.

"No," I said. Why hadn't I noticed the clues? Why hadn't Bryan? The way he acted when we talked about her; how he'd been keeping a low profile after Payne's murder; his reactions to Cassandra when she came to the ball game . . .

Had she come to the game to see him, or me?

"How long had you been . . . seeing her?" I asked.

"Three or four months. I'm not even sure how it happened. It just did," he said. He now sat down, across from me.

I knew what he meant.

"She didn't want to see me anymore," David went on. "She said because of her husband, if he ever found out, all a bunch of crap. I suggested that maybe if he were to disappear, maybe we could be together. 'Maybe,' she said. I said I'd kill him for her. She didn't think I was serious. But I was serious."

"So you did it."

"I don't know what I was thinking. I bought a gun. I waited for him at the airport. I followed the cab. I pulled up alongside the cab . . . I was crazy."

Part of Bryan's theory was right.

"You did all this for that woman?" I said. "For—"

"Didn't *you*?"

He had me there.

We were silent for the longest minute.

"So what now," he said.

"What now," I said, holding up my hands.

"Will you turn me in?"

"I'm done with this whole fucking thing," I told him. "You do whatever you feel is the right thing to do."

"I should turn myself in," he said.

The truth is, I wanted to kill him. I wanted to jump up, grab him by the neck, and take his life for the mess he'd caused. He started the ball rolling. If he hadn't killed Payne, many people would be alive, including Jessica and Bryan.

I didn't have it in me to even move.

"Do what you feel is right," I said.

David nodded and left.

He never turned himself in. He drove out to the Anza-

Borrego desert, a good sixty miles from the city, and put a bullet in his head, with the same gun he'd used to shoot Payne. His body wasn't found for weeks, but the police didn't put it together. He left a note in his car. It said: *Jellyfish*. Who knew what that meant. The cops decided it meant nothing.

I could've solved everything for the cops, but I had too much to risk. I was connected to a lot of dead bodies in Las Vegas. I'd have to answer too many questions, I'd have to reveal too many secrets. After a while, Vegas seemed too weird to be real, and I started to become skeptical about the accuracy of my memory.

I just wanted to be done with all this.

The following days I spent enduring the untidy, ugly, and sad business of saying good-bye to the dead. First, there was my daughter's funeral. Tina wore black, her face veiled, and Matthew wore a black suit. Neither one of them spoke to me. This didn't surprise me, and it didn't hurt. I was a hollow thing. Members of both our families didn't ostracize me—for which I was both thankful and weary of. Had Tina said anything to anyone? Did anyone know that I was with someone else while my son set the fire and my daughter ran into the street? The day after we buried Jessica, I was served with divorce papers by Tina's lawyer. I called the lawyer (thankfully it was someone in my former profession that I didn't know) and told him I wouldn't give a fight, I wanted to make it a clean divorce, Tina could have whatever she wanted. The lawyer, pleased to hear this, told me that Tina only wanted half of our money and property, and wanted me to foot the bill for Matthew's psychiatric care. I said fine. He also informed me that a wrongful death suit had been filed against the city regarding Jessica's death, and he was certain the city would quickly settle, and that Tina didn't want me to make a claim on whatever money she collected from that settlement. I said this was fine as well.

Bryan's funeral was next. Tina was there, again in black, and again, she did not speak to me or acknowledge my presence.

I couldn't sleep in the house, I couldn't even stay another second. It was going to be put up for sale anyway. I was going to rent an apartment, or maybe just a room somewhere downtown.

If the police suspected Cassandra of anything, I would never know. They did investigate Bryan's murder—asking me questions about the man who'd shot him. I knew other investigations were going on in Nevada. Would they eventually piece it all together? I expected the police—or the FBI or the Treasury Department—to show up and haul me away one of these days. They'd found the Mustang and Rook's body, as well as the body of a young woman and two men, and Boyd's body in the motel room . . . all connected to the bodies of five federal agents in an abandoned casino . . . all connected to a dead banker and cab driver . . . connected to a dead ex-cop and a little girl . . . and finally me.

They never came. Not then, and not to this day.

The only thing I can figure, someone cleaned up the mess in Las Vegas.

What I did get was a letter from Cassandra Payne. It read: *Take the money, save it, and send your son to college, do something useful with it.*

Enclosed was a cashier's check for thirty thousand dollars. The same amount she'd spent to have her husband removed from her life. The check was issued from a bank in New Jersey, the envelope postmarked from New York City.

Eventually, I cashed the check. I placed ten thousand in a trust fund for Matthew. He wouldn't be able to touch it until he was twenty-one, unless he was enrolled in college. That was my stipulation. It was so very far in the future, I realized.

As for the rest, it was a good sum with which to try and start my life over. I talked myself into believing that I deserved the twenty thousand, and that Cassandra Payne owed it to me to help me begin a new life, since she was instrumental—whether she acknowledged her part or not—in destroying my old one.

I called my lawyer acquaintance, Ray McCann, and asked him if he recalled our conversation at the barbecue party, when he was drunk, offering me a job doing paralegal or investigative work.

"Well, um," he said, "ah . . ."

"Don't worry, Ray. I'm not calling for a job. I was wondering if you knew any good private investigators."

"Oh," he said, "there's a couple I've worked with."

"I need to hire one."

"Oh. Well, yes. I can refer you to this one fellow."

I hired a young private eye named Desmond Bell. I gave him all the information I had on Rachel Vaughn—last known residence in Chicago, twenty-nine or thirty years old. This was all Bryan had given me. The PI conceded that it wasn't a lot, but he'd give it a try. He found her in two weeks. She was living in Portland, Oregon, where she worked as a waitress in a diner.

I went to Portland.

I sat in the all-night diner. It was 7 P.M. I had a hamburger, was nibbling at it. My waitress's name tag read RACHEL. She was a little plump, with dyed red hair pulled back. I could see Bryan's features on her.

She gave me my check.

"Rachel."

"Yeah."

"Would you sit down with me? Can we talk?"

"Don't waste your time," she said. "I just got divorced and I've sworn off men."

"It's not that," I said. "I'd like to talk to you about your father."

She frowned. "Say what?"

"Bryan Vaughn. He was your father?"

"Who the fuck are you?" She raised her voice, took a step back.

"It's all right," I said quickly. "I was a friend of your father's. We were—neighbors. He passed away two months ago."

She opened her mouth. She didn't say anything. Her eyes got big and several tears fell down her face. She sat across from me.

"He's dead?"

"Yes," I said.

"How?"

"He was shot."

"In the line of duty?"

"No. He was retired from the force."

"How did he get shot?"

"It's a long story."

"How do I know you're not lying? What's my mother's name?"

"Ellen. She's a librarian."

Rachel nodded.

I said, "Your father, before he died, wanted me to find you."

"How is my mother?" she asked.

"She's okay," I said, although I knew she wasn't.

"I get off in an hour," Rachel said. "Will you wait for me? We'll go get a drink and talk."

I watched her finish her shift, moving zombielike, an automaton filling coffee cups and taking orders. I wondered what she was thinking, what was going on inside her? I felt very sad.

We went across the street to a bar. She had a beer, I had water. We sat in a small and dark booth. There weren't very many people in the bar.

I told her the story—not the whole story, of course, but what she needed to know.

She listened, and looked sad in a hard kind of way. I could see a lot of pain pushed back on her face. Not just the pain of the news but other pain.

She told me it had never been her intention to stay out of touch with her parents this long. She didn't want to look back, she wanted to reshape her life, her history, forget that she had a policeman for a father, a weak woman for a mother, and a sister that had killed herself. She wanted to call home, or go home, but the past ten years had been one failure after another—she'd been married and divorced twice, had one stillbirth, and had been a heroin addict for two years but was now clean. She was thirty and barely supporting herself waiting tables. She was ashamed, she told me; she didn't want her parents to know what a pathetic life she'd led.

"I understand," I said.

"The hell you do," she said.

"I do," I said.

She studied my face. "I think you do."

I decided to have a beer. I told her about the months during which her father and I would drink beer and sit around and chat. I told her Bryan loved her, had always love her. I told her that her mother needed her.

"Wait, stop," she said, holding out a hand, looking away. "This is too much for me. Okay? This is too much right now."

I walked her home. She had an apartment ten blocks away. It was starting to rain. She invited me inside. Now that we were not in a public place she started to cry, to really let it out. I held her to me, I let her cry onto my chest.

23

Seven weeks later, I moved up to Seattle and rented a house. Rachel moved in with me. We had taken a trip back to San Diego, where she was reunited with her mother. I think Ellen knew what was going on between us, and I think she was happy. A year later, when we told Ellen we were getting married, she gave us her blessing.

We had a quiet wedding, with Ellen and a few friends in Seattle attending.

We moved to Tallahassee, Florida. I don't know why. Maybe to get away from all the rain. Maybe because the weather was like San Diego. Rachel got a job at a real estate firm, and I took—and passed—the Florida State Bar. I was an attorney again. I got a job at the public defender's office, just like I'd done the first time around.

Rachel was pregnant in our third year of marriage. We had a daughter and named her Brianna.

As for Matthew, despite therapy, he continued to set fires. He set a big one, and was placed in a juvenile detention center. When I told Tina I was getting remarried, all she said was, "Be good to her. Don't fuck around on her like you did to me."

I wanted to tell Rachel the real story, the whole story. But I knew she wouldn't believe it. And after a while, I didn't see the point. I wouldn't have believed it either.

Two years later—five years after Las Vegas—I chanced upon Cassandra Payne at the JFK Airport.

I was in New York to depose a witness; it was a high-profile case in Florida that could make or break my career as a defense attorney. I was waiting for my flight, and in one of the bars I saw a woman—from the corner of my eye—who looked like someone I knew.

I approached her. She was at the counter, drinking a bourbon on the rocks. She wore a long dark skirt with a high slit on one side, and a white blouse. Her black hair was the same, parted in the middle. Her perfume was the same—and I felt five years younger, and I was scared.

Oh yes, I was scared.

"Cassandra?"

She turned. She smiled. "Well, Mr. Lansdale."

I didn't know what to do—hug her, kiss her on the cheek. What would be the proper move? I didn't do anything. I found myself staring at her thick, dark eyebrows, and remembering more: feeling things I didn't want to feel.

She wasn't the least bit fazed by my presence. "What brings you to New York?" she said.

"Business, leaving," I replied.

She looked just the same, but I was different—ten pounds heavier, receding hairline. At least I had a Florida tan.

"I'm leaving too," she said.

"But you live here now? In New York," I questioned, recalling the postmark on the letter she sent.

She didn't acknowledge that. She asked, "How have you been?"

There was so much I wanted to tell her. I'd thought often of this day, when I could report to her what my life had become after our experience together, the use that I'd made of the money she sent, that I had another daughter now (a day didn't go by that I didn't think of little Jessica, and the plastic dinosaurs she loved so dearly).

Before I could utter a word, we were joined by a tall, handsome man with slicked-back dark hair. He looked to be in his mid-twenties. His teeth were very even and white. He wore a sharp pin-striped suit, the kind you'd expect a stockbroker or banker to wear.

"Dear," she said to the man, "this is Mr. Philip Lansdale. We used to know each other—we used to be next-door neighbors once, believe it or not."

"Oh," he said. "A weird coincidence, meeting *here*, I bet." He had a New York accent. I had a feeling he *was* a stockbroker.

"It happens sometimes," she said.

"Synchronicity?" he asked her.

"That has to do with events," she told him. "This is a chance encounter."

"Joe Greynard," he said to me. "Cassandra's husband." He held out his hand. I shook hands with him, and looked into his pretty blue eyes. I understood that he didn't know a thing.

"Nice to meet you," I said.

"Well, we should get going," he said to his wife. "Our plane's boarding."

"We're off to Barbados," Cassandra said.

"Much needed vacation," her husband added.

"I hope you have a nice trip," I said.

"Thank you," he said.

"It was nice seeing you again, Mr. Lansdale," Cassandra said.

"You too—Mrs. Greynard," I said.

"Cheerio," she said, with intention, licking her lips. She looked at her drink, and then me.

They walked out of the bar. Cassandra turned, and smiled; it was a quick motion, something her husband didn't notice. I smiled back.

Yes, we shared a big secret. We always would.

Her glass was half-full. I drank what was left. It tasted like a night long ago, of forbidden lust and outlandish terror.

I waved at the bartender and ordered another Wild Turkey on the rocks.